A Small Hotel

A Small Hotel

ROBERT OLEN BUTLER

Grove Press
New York

Published simultaneously in Canada
Printed in the United States of America

ISBN-13: 978-0-8021-1987-2

Grove Press
an imprint of Grove/Atlantic, Inc.
841 Broadway
New York, NY 10003

Distributed by Publishers Group West

www.groveatlantic.com

11 12 13 14   10 9 8 7 6 5 4 3 2 1

For my agent and friend,
Warren Frazier

Acknowledgments

I offer my sincere thanks to the folks at both the Olivier House Hotel and Oak Alley Plantation for their kind assistance in my preparations for this book. These have long been two of my favorite places in the New Orleans area, for their history and for their aesthetics and for the intelligence, helpfulness and downright charm of the staffs. Needless to say, any characters in this novel associated with those two places are strictly fictional, products of the artistic necessities of the book, and have no real-life counterparts.

A Small
Hotel

On the afternoon of the day when she fails to show up in a judge's chambers in Pensacola to finalize her divorce, Kelly Hays swerves her basic-black Mercedes into the valet spot and thumps hard into the curb and pops the gearshift into park, and then she feels a silence rush through her chest and limbs and mind that should terrify her. But she yields herself to it. She brings her face forward and lays her forehead gently against the steering wheel. She sits in front of the Olivier House on Toulouse Street in the New Orleans French Quarter, a hotel she knows quite well. Like this present silence overcoming the welter in her, before she stepped from her house in Pensacola a little over three hours ago she yanked her hair back into a ponytail and simply stroked a hasty touch of lipstick onto her lips but she then was moved to put on her favorite little black dress, a sleeveless sheath, a prêt-à-porter Chanel she'd had for years, put it on slowly in the muffled silence of her walk-in closet, listening to the Chanel's faint rustle going over her, letting the silk lick her down the thighs. She turned forty-nine years old two months ago on her deck, alone with a single-malt, looking out at the Bayou Texar going dark in the twilight. She wore makeup that night, for herself, prompted by the Scotch, and she wore her hair in a French twist, and she knew, in spite of everything, that she looked thirty-something, even early-thirty-something. And she knows now that she looks all of forty-nine. All and more as the door to her car opens and she lifts her face to a gaunt, long-jawed, middle-aged man, a man she recognizes.

He recognizes her, too. "Ah," he says. "Welcome back, Mrs . . ." and he snags on her name, even as she forces her body to turn, forces her feet to the pavement outside, and she rises from the seat.

She sees him duck a little, to check out the passenger side of the car. He is looking for her husband.

"If you can just take care of the car," she says, wanting only to stop any small talk, wanting only to close the door behind her in her room.

"I'm sorry," the man says. "I used to be better at names."

"Beau, isn't it?"

"Beau. Yes. Thanks for remembering. I used to be better at that." And he steps to the rear of the car, seeing her small Gucci upright bag lying in the back seat. He reaches for the door handle.

"Beau," Kelly says, firmly, "I can handle my bag. Just do the car."

Beau withdraws his hand. "The car," he says. "Sure."

"I'm sorry," Kelly says. "Hays."

"Mrs. Hays," Beau says, brightening. "Of course. Glad to have you back."

And now she stops on the sidewalk before the door to the hotel, and she lets go of the handle of her rolling bag. She can turn and stop Beau, who has only this moment closed the driver door of the car, she can stop him and she can get back into her car and drive away. Ah, but to where. To the house. To Hell with the house. She doesn't want the house. Someone laughs down the street.

She turns to look. It is a small sound from this distance, but she heard it clearly. A young man and a young woman lean into each other at the door of a bar at the corner of Bourbon Street. She knows the bar, too. The young couple in this moment and perhaps the bar twenty-five years ago and half a dozen times since: these are things she can consider. But nothing else for now. The rest is carefully put away. The rest is inside the bag, whose handle she now grasps. She will go in. And she does. She goes up the steps and through the door into the Olivier House, an early nineteenth-century townhouse with a Federal façade of plastered brick and a labyrinthine Creole inner life with loggias and two courtyards and slave quarters and four floors of galleried rooms.

And she is at the end of the entrance hall, near the parlor door, and she is glad the young man at the desk is a stranger and she has her key and is through the double doors behind him and crossing a small flagstone courtyard rimmed in banana trees and fig trees and she is through a low, curving loggia and into the larger courtyard with the swimming pool, but she turns at once up a staircase and she climbs one floor and another and she is breathless now, not from the climb but from the room before her.

Room 303. Two narrow black doors, each with three stacked panes of glass: fully half the doors are glass, and it surprises her; this is a thing she should remember well but she doesn't. The doors are hung with white ruffled curtains, and her hand jitters the key against the lock, unable to get it into the hole. She stops. She lowers her hand. She wants in badly, wants into this room that she came to feel was her own place in the Quarter. No. She always felt it was *their* place. But hers now. Entirely hers. And she wants in so badly that she cannot get in, from the very wanting of it. She breathes deeply. She raises her hand again and focuses on keeping it steady, and at last the key slips into the lock and the door is opening and she is inside and the door shuts behind her. She lets go of her bag. She closes her eyes.

The smell of the place is always the same. Old wood and old rugs and fresh sheets and from the open balcony doors the sweet but tainted smell of the Quarter, jasmine and roux and shellfish brine, beer and piss and mildew, and something of the river too, and the swamp, and a hard rain that passed by, and ozone and coffee and sex, Michael's smells and her smells: can all of this be inside her in this room in this moment? Probably. She is weeping.

~

And as Kelly lets the tears fall without even lifting a hand to them, the man she is still married to is across the Mississippi, driving fast, an hour west of New Orleans along Louisiana 18. On one side is the river, invisible behind the berm of the levee, and on the other side has been a run of tank farms and cane fields and strip malls and swamp, and Creole plantations too—Laura and St. Joseph and, at last, Oak Alley. Michael Hays slows his BMW. He put the top down when they crossed the cantilever bridge into the West Bank and took to the state two-lanes, and he has glanced at the woman beside him half a dozen times since then, watched her hair: she has tied it up tightly in a scarf but some tendrils have gotten free and are flaring behind her, a pallid yellow flame. Michael is fifty-five. The woman beside him, Laurie Pruitt, when she tells anyone of her boyfriend, which she has begun now to do—a few select friends, her mother—she told her mother last week and is determined never to speak of him to her again—Laurie always describes him as "a handsomely ripening fifty-five." She is twenty-nine. Michael has timed his glances from his periphery so she never sees him. He wishes simply to collect these snapshots of her. He has stifled even the impulse—which is strong in him—to reach out his hand and put it in this flame of her hair. If it could actually burn him, he might. A strong assault of feeling: this he could take. But not the gentle thing, though he knows this weekend at Oak Alley will inevitably bring that too. But waiting for word from Pensacola, he has stayed bound tightly inside himself.

Before them now is the quarter-mile alley of live oaks leading from the highway to the Big House, and Michael slows even more. He and Laurie both turn their heads, as they slide past, to look down the canopied corridor of trees. With the massive frame of the oaks, the Creole pavilion house shows only its wide, double-galleried face, fronted by two-story Tuscan columns, and then it is gone. And momentarily Michael slows almost to a stop and turns into the plantation grounds, passing a sign that announces: *Antebellum Fashion Festival*.

Before he accelerates again, Laurie says, "I wish we'd begun a year earlier."

He has had these what-can-you-possibly-be-thinking moments several times already with her. The wreckage he is leaving behind was inconveniently timed? He will not let her remark make him consider the wreckage now. And it is deeply in his nature not to make his inner life visible. So he shows nothing. If she looked at him, Laurie would not be able to tell if he even heard what she said. Not that this occurs to her. After only a moment's pause, she says, "There are twenty-eight oaks and twenty-eight columns around the house. It would be cool if I were twenty-eight this first time." He speeds up now on the perimeter road and she has said what she has to say, more for herself than for Michael, and that he makes no indication whatsoever he has heard is of no consequence to her. The Big House emerges fully as they run parallel to the alley of oaks, its dark, hipped roof rising to a widow's walk.

~

And Kelly is standing in the center of Room 303, at
the foot of the four-poster double bed, with the posts
and the canopy frame and two birds plucking at an
overflowing basket of grapes on the headboard all done
in black wrought iron. This and so many other things
are as they always have been. The bed wall is exposed
brick. The lamp on the night table is a sandalwood palm
tree. The lamp on the desk on the opposite wall is a teak
monkey in a fez, climbing another palm. He is draped
with Mardi Gras beads. The beads may have changed
over the years, but there have always been beads. The
French windows are open to a trompe l'oeil balcony,
a filigreed iron balustrade from one side of the jamb
to the other. Nowhere to step outside. Just lean there
and look down to the courtyard and out to the hipped
and gabled roofs of the Quarter and to the sun, falling
toward late afternoon in the western sky before her.

Laughter wafts into the room like a fresh scent
from the street. Kelly leaves her bag behind and moves
to the balcony. She looks down. In an open doorway
to one of the pool-level suites, a young couple laughs
and the woman nudges the man's shoulder with her
forehead and he says something else and she lifts her
face and laughs harder, though the sound strikes Kelly's
ear only faintly, as faint as distant memory; the laughter
has sounded in her enough to have drawn her to look

but not enough to dissipate the murk in her head, her chest. She turns away, faces back into the room.

She looks at her bag sitting upright on the floor, its handle extended. She moves to the bag, grasps the handle. The laughter dies. She lifts her eyes to the door of the room. Outside, she herself waits to enter. Kelly at twenty-four. Perhaps the age of the woman in the courtyard. But Kelly in this present moment, holding tight at the handle of her rolling bag, squeezes back the memory, keeps the door shut. She angles the bag toward her, turns, pulls it to the side of the bed. She lowers the handle and bends and lifts the bag and places it gently on the mattress. She is breathing heavily, though the bag was light. She waits. She slows herself down. There is time yet. Perhaps even options of a sort. This whole process is to do one thing and then wait and then do another thing.

For now, open the bag: the zipper tab between her thumb and forefinger, the ripping sound, her hand tracing the bag, down and across and up. And she lifts the lid. Inside is a folded, bulky, white terry-cloth robe. But it is here only for padding. She unfolds the robe, and within are simply a bottle of Macallan cask-strength, single-malt Scotch and a bottle of Percocet.

~

Michael steps from his car into the driveway next to a pitched-roof cottage with a screened front porch and a wooden back deck. Surrounding the plantation grounds is the ongoing enterprise of the last hundred and seventy years at Oak Alley, sugarcane. The air still smells faintly of smoke and cane, the fall harvest having been completed only a short time ago, the crop cut and gone for processing and the stubble burned to the ground, leaving six hundred acres of dark rutted earth waiting for the new shoots. Michael takes in the smell, a pleasure he had not expected this weekend.

"It's wonderful," Laurie says. "More than I'd imagined."

Michael does not look at her but heads toward the trunk, lifting her Rollaboard from the back seat as he passes. He takes one step beyond the end of the car and puts her rolling bag on the driveway for her to pull. She's in the small front yard, her back to him, arms rising as if embracing the scene before her: another cottage on the service road and a maintenance shop farther out and then five hundred yards of naked cane fields to a distant line of trees marking an unseen railroad track. Her arms move on, though, and she clasps her hands at the back of her head. Her shoulders lift and pause and fall in a sweet sigh of contentment.

Michael doesn't see it. One by one he pulls Laurie's suitcase and a mate to Kelly's upright bag and his garment carrier out of the trunk, setting the larger bags beside each other and draping the garment bag over Laurie's suitcase.

He turns to close the trunk and she is beside him now. "Thanks for letting me choose this place," she says.

He lowers the trunk and gently clicks it shut. He turns to her and she is kissing him hard on the mouth and he is fine with bodies, fine with using the language of the body, and he presses her close and the kiss goes on and then ends and they break. Laurie looks Michael in the eyes.

She says, "Now that's way too somber a look after a kiss like that." She cocks her head slightly. "Don't you think?"

And he clenches inside. What more does she want from him? He is a man of words in the courtroom, this Michael Hays. But the expectation of words in a circumstance like this always makes him take the Fifth—silently—no matter what those words might be if he were inclined to figure them out. So instead, suddenly clumsy even with his body, he kisses her again, trying for the forehead—given his putoffedness—but his incipient move prompts her to raise her face to him, as she assumes he's after her lips. Consequently, he ends up kissing her high on the bridge of her nose. Which gives even the usually chilled-out Laurie her own what-can-you-possibly-be-thinking moment.

But now they are pulling their luggage along, and she has taken his garment bag over her arm without his even asking, and they are through the porch door and the cottage door and moving through their living room full of cherrywood Chippendale reproductions, and Laurie leads the way into the dining room and then, to the right, into a hallway that leads back toward the front of the cottage and into the master bedroom. The bed is large, mahogany, the four high, fluted posts with carved rice plants. She stops, leaves the luggage on the floor, moves around the corner of the foot of the bed with one hand on the post like a stripper doing a slow turn on her pole.

He has stopped, blocked by the bags on the floor.

"I love it," she says. "I love it all."

She puts her hand now on the floral chintz quilt. But she pauses and straightens and looks at Michael. "Of course," she says. "Now I get your mood. Duh."

She does not elaborate, and Michael looks at her and suppresses a bristling at her trying to read his mood. She has cocked her head at him. He waits for more.

"You were here with her," she says.

He leaves the upright where it sits and collapses the rolling handle of Laurie's suitcase. He lifts the bag. He finds the heft of the thing a comfort at the moment: the physical focus helps him stop the memories. He steps around the bags on the floor and puts the suitcase on the luggage stand by the dresser.

"Did you come for the festival?" Laurie says.

He turns back to the other bags and she twirls on the bedpost again, once, and heads for him. He stops, straightens, waits.

"Did she dress up?" she says.

"No," he says.

She is before him now. Smiling very slightly at one corner of her mouth. Smelling of something with patchouli that Kelly used to wear. "So I'll be your first Scarlett," Laurie says.

"Frankly, my dear, I don't give a damn," Michael says, sounding harsher than he wants, in spite of this being, prima facie, a joke.

Laurie misses the allusion for the briefest of moments. His tone is flat. This is Michael, after all, whose silences and hard edges she is still trying to figure out, thinking he's worth it, thinking this is a real man, not another overgrown boy. But the ongoing mystery of him means that in spite of her having introduced the frame of reference, she needs a moment to realize he's just quoted an actual line from her favorite movie in the whole world of all time. She laughs. "My heard-hearted Rhett," she says.

He thinks to try but he can't make himself unloosen his tone, not with his struggle to remain in this moment, with just Laurie. "Let me unpack the bags," he says. "Not the baggage."

She studies his face. He's the trial lawyer who has just sprung a little rhetorical trap and is playing it deadpan. She lifts her hand and extends her forefinger and puts the tip of it on the tip of his nose. She pushes, gently. He lets her do it.

"I'm for that," she says. She turns away.

With her back to him now, Michael finds himself very conscious of the tip of his nose. He needed to make the point: for Laurie's sake as well as his own, he can't let Kelly into this room. But the tip of his nose makes him smile a faint, tender, involuntary smile at Laurie. A smile that she cannot see. And in this moment of Michael's letting go to a gentle thing, Kelly spins to him in the center of an Oak Alley cottage bedroom, perhaps this very one, spins to him and leaps into his arms, leaps and hooks her legs around him. This was early on, in their first six months or so. Before they'd married. Before they'd even spoken of marrying. She was younger than Laurie is now, younger by five years.

Kelly leapt into his arms and they kissed, and the kiss ended, and still she clung to him, and he carried her toward the bed, and she said, "Not yet," and she began to hum. Michael has lost the tune over the years but he clearly remembers her humming, and he moved back to the center of the floor with her holding fast to him and the song she hummed was a waltz. Yes. That much still clings to this memory. A waltz, and he began to do the steps. He waltzed her around this room, around and around this room to the music she hummed softly in his ear, and he was glad that her head was pressed hard against the side of his because the last thing in the world he wanted was to let this woman he loved see tears in his eyes. It makes no difference that they were happy tears. Tears are tears. And he held her tight even after the music stopped. He pressed her close even when he felt her begin to try to straighten up to look him in the face. He held her closer, and she seemed happy to just settle back in, and he held her like that until his tears dried on their own and she would never know.

~

Kelly closes her bag. Zips it. Pulls it off the bed and steps toward the corner of the room to put the bag out of the way. On the night table sit the bottle of Scotch and the bottle of pills. She has moved the lamp to the far side of the tabletop, next to the clock radio, and she has placed the two bottles carefully side by side in the center of the empty space, their labels facing the bed. She has turned the clock face away, though she has carefully made the radio's edges parallel with the tabletop. And she moves past all this now without a glance and she stops in the center of the floor at the foot of the bed and she stands very still and she is seeing nothing at all around her and she is feeling that silence again, but this time it has not rushed into her, she just realizes it's there, filling her up. Her arms hang at her sides and she cannot imagine lifting them.

But she does see the door now. And Kelly does let Kelly into the room. Kelly at twenty-four. The door opens and she steps in. She is wearing black stiletto boots and black leggings and a black mock-turtle tee and black cat ears. Her black mask is gone so she can cry, and her painted cat whiskers are streaked down her cheeks from tears that have only recently stopped. An arm's length behind her is Michael. Thirty years old in this memory. He is wearing a Tulane Law sweatshirt. Both of them have strands of gold and purple and green beads around their necks. The French windows are closed but the muffled din of Mardi Gras fills the room like the smell of cigarette smoke in the bedding.

Kelly takes only one more step and stops. It's his room. She is trembling. She feels him come near her, though there is no touching. She senses him as you might sense a live oak in the pitch dark. She waits for him to put his arms around her. She wants that. But he does not touch her. And she wants that too, wants this to be how he is. He rescued her in the midst of Mardi Gras, but having done it, he does not touch her. Not yet. These are, however, not things she is thinking about. These things are simply playing in her body, alongside the trembling.

"I'm sorry," she says.

"That was scary for you," Michael says.

She turns to him. His eyes are the color of that oak in the dark. The trembling is bad and it's time to be held. She knows this and he must too, because all at once she is in his arms and clinging to him, though she is aware how he holds his body back a little, holds her only with his arms and his chest and she likes him even more for this and she clings harder.

Her head is upon his chest and from there she says, "I don't even know your name to thank you."

"Michael Hays."

"I'm ..." she begins.

But he cuts her off. "Catwoman. I know. I've admired your work."

She pulls away a little to look at him, though they keep their arms around each other. "You mean you don't favor that little shit in the bat costume?" she says.

"Please," he says. "I'm a lawyer."

She wants to laugh but things are still roiling in her. "Sorry. I just can't stop shaking."

"I know."

"It's not that you're a lawyer."

"Good," Michael says.

She puts her head back on his chest. "Kelly Dillard," she says.

He does not reply.

"You didn't know my name either," she says.

"Kelly Dillard," he says. "You're safe now."

And Kelly twenty-five years later breaks off the memory. The pulse of strength it takes to do this lets her lift an arm, draw her wrist across her forehead, which is moist from the warm, muggy late October that has pushed itself into her room. She thinks to close the French windows, thinks this to stop thinking anything else. Not now, she decides. She'll keep them open. The courtyard below is silent. But is that someone laughing? Perhaps. Far off this time. Out in the Quarter somewhere. Perhaps. But it's done now. She is managing her mind now.

She moves to the side of the bed and sits. She turns her face to the night table. The Scotch is a deep amber and she looks closely at the Jacobean manor house on the label, a holly tree next to it, nearly as tall as the top of the pitched roof. This house must exist somewhere, she thinks. Two hundred years ago a woman stood at that third-floor window and looked out on her lawn and thought she could use a drink, could really use a nice old Scotch to burn her tongue. I could use a drink, Kelly thinks. But instead, there is laughter again somewhere. And Kelly's mind resumes managing itself. She needs to go back to the way this all began between her and Michael, from the start, from the time when Michael was nearby but they had no idea each other even existed, when the smallest impulse in her—for a drink, for a pee—would have put her in a slightly different place at a slightly different time and her life would have been profoundly changed forever.

She is standing outside the bar at the corner of Toulouse and Bourbon and there is laughter and shouting and a great gabbling roar of voices and Bourbon Street is tightly thronged and it is that first Mardi Gras and her black mask is still on and her whiskers are still pristine and she does not yet know Michael Hays exists in the world, and her sister Katie, four years older and

the prime instigator of this visit, and Theresa, Katie's
life-long friend—the reassuringly-even-more-messed-
up-than-I-am sort of friend—are huddled with her as
shirtless frat boy revelers painted gold and purple lurch
past, and Katie says in a shout above the din, "My head's
about to explode."

Theresa says, "Definitely time for a pit stop."

And now more frat boys. Maybe frat boys. Three
of them, young certainly, not painted but drunk. They
float by and they make meowing sounds at Kelly and
veer too near her and she turns her back to them and
they go on. Theresa says to her, "I should have done
like you. I need a costume." Both Theresa and Katie
are dressed in jeans and sweatshirts.

"I need a drink," Katie says.

"Me too," Theresa says.

Katie does a now-presenting hand-sweep toward
the door nearby. "Bar," she says.

"Bar," Theresa says.

The sound of the crowd swells down the block.
This is all still new to Kelly and she is not drunk and
she has no need to get drunk at the moment. She feels
surprisingly invisible here and she wonders if that's one
of the allures of Mardi Gras, to feel this way: unseen,
unseeable, unknowable in the midst of the tumult of so
many others. And the more intense the crowd, the more

comfortably bound inside herself she feels. The crowd down Bourbon is chanting something and cheering and Kelly says, "You two go on in. I'll catch up with you in a few minutes."

"You going to flash for some real beads?" Theresa says.

"Catwoman's above all that," Kelly says, and she moves off toward the hubbub.

People are packed too densely for her to push through in the street itself so she moves to the edge of the sidewalk, just beneath the overhanging balconies, finding the seam between the street crowd and the crowd that has oozed from the doors of bars and clubs. Underfoot is the squinch and slide of the gutter muck and the smells are strong of waste and spillage and spew, smells that will become for Kelly, in the years ahead, just a faint presence in the nose and in the finish of the scent of New Orleans, a not unpleasant thing in that form, like the smell of a skunk from a great distance out on a farm road can be not unpleasant, but near to her, in her first Mardi Gras, the smell is overwhelming and she struggles to keep her footing in her stilettos. But she makes progress toward the voluble center of the block.

Voluble now with a cry in unison: "Show your tits! Show your tits!" Over and over the cry is sent upwards

and Kelly is facing this compressed center of the crowd
and she is beneath a wide Creole townhouse balcony
with the objects of the crowd's attention clearly located
above. All eyes are turned upward, a hundred hands are
raised, jiggling strands of beads. And right in front of her
is a small cleared arc of space made by the crowd having
moved away a bit from two young women. These two
are the objects of a quieter entreaty from above. They
are each of them a little too corpulent, not quite pretty
in the face, one with a weak chin and a crooked nose,
the other with close set eyes and thin lips, not homely
but not quite pretty, women who never get looked at
twice in the Florida town or the South Carolina town
or the Illinois town where they live, but here they
wear tank tops and they are the objects of intense and
clamorous interest, and these bodies of theirs, which
they stand before mirrors and criticize and rue for all
the other days of the year, are suddenly desirable, are
commodities of great value commanding a currency
that everyone around them covets ardently, the beads,
the good beads, the thick red and gold and purple and
green beads with attachments, with miniature masks
or babies or mermaids or devils or rubber duckies or
bottles of Jim Beam, cheap shit novelty stuff at any
other time of the year but on these few days they are
the world's wealth, they are physical objects of desire,

they are the primo Mardi Gras throws, and the two young women can have these things because of their bodies and they can have wild adulation from faces and cameras and whoopings and cheers all around them, but first there is negotiation, there is naked capitalism, supply and demand, hard bargaining. And Kelly takes all this in and her sense of being alone here in the middle of this tumult, alone and untouchable in her own solitude, is very strong now.

And the crowd cheers and the air is full of beads flying up, up and out of sight toward the balcony and caught above: tits have been shown up there just now and the two young women in the street are laughing and they look at each other and Kelly takes a step into the empty space, away from the two women but near them, she stands with those who are gawking and pleading, and she glances up, and all along the balcony is a row of mostly male faces turned downwards. But side by side in the center of the row are two young women and they are putting on their new beads, their nipples blinkered again somewhere beneath the dozens of heavy strands of accumulated wealth.

And next to the women who flashed are two men with forearms draped in large-beaded plastic necklaces. Gold ones with the beads alternating three to one with black Darth Vader heads and purple ones with jester

faces and another with king cake babies and another
with a Big Bird pendant, and the men dangle these
now at the two women before Kelly. She looks at them.
The women are motioning to the beads they want.
The business of this goes forward. They are demanding two strands. Not two for the two of them. Two
for each of them. The man above is not giving in. The
women gesture: one strand for each tit. He appreciates
the argument, but he will not yield. One for each set.
And the crowd is now joining in the negotiation. The
faces have all turned to the two women from Panama
City or from Aiken or from Joliet and they are secretar-
ies in a real estate office or they are elementary school
teachers or they are librarians and the crowd is crying
out to them "Show your tits! Show your tits!" and the
most wonderful beads are quivering above them and
they look at each other and they laugh and they know
that they are, in this moment, something they always
dreamed they might be, and they raise their faces and
grasp the bottoms of their tank tops and they lift the
tops and their breasts are naked in New Orleans, their
nipples wake wide-eyed to the pop of flashbulbs and
the loud cheers of hundreds.

And Kelly, fascinated thus far, now recoils inside,
once she sees the deal being closed. She never quite
indentified with the two young women. She is herself

pretty, pretty enough and confident enough in her prettiness not to have that particular self-doubt, and the self-doubt she cannot name but that fills her up could never be assuaged by strangers, and she knows the value of the objects in the world and she desires many of them but not if Big Bird or Darth Vader are attached, not even in this sealed, self-defining world of Mardi Gras, because she has felt for a little while here that she is herself sealed and self-defining, but now it's time to move away, go back to the bar and have a drink with her sister and her friend.

But the crowd is shifting its focus, and Kelly finds that the two young women are sliding away and she has a sudden empty space around her and the way back to the sidewalk has new faces, new bodies, men who are focused on Kelly now and are shoulder-to-shoulder and she doesn't want to have to push by them and she has a quick sharp-clawed scrabbling in her chest and she can hear a call of "Catwoman" from above and she looks up and one of the young men is dangling a long strand of purple beads with a Batman pendant and he makes a lifting motion for her to show her tits and the man next to him is making the same gesture and the two balcony women are laughing and dipping their heads at Kelly in encouragement and they pantomime the raising of their own tops and Kelly shakes her head no, not me, I won't, and she turns, looking for a way out, she makes a complete circle, looking for a way out but seeing only the tightly compacted crowd, and all the faces are on her and the cameras are raised and the circle she makes does not look to anyone like panic and the urge to flee, it looks like a show, like an appeal for encouragement, and the crowd takes that up with the cry of "Show your tits! Show your tits!"

Kelly might as well be totally naked, right now, right where she stands, her skin prickles with vulnerability and her limbs are crazy restless and the men blocking the sidewalk are scarier to her, more personal, than the street crowd, and she turns around once more, decided already that she has no choice but to lunge toward these very voices demanding her nakedness, and she raises her hands before her and lowers her face and she throws herself forward and she will pummel and weep and press her way out of this space no matter what.

And the crowd parts at once, swallowing Kelly into its midst, and more women slide into the marketplace behind her and the crowd instantly shifts its attention and forgets why they absorbed this woman in black so readily and she is trapped again, tightly bound in by bodies on all sides in the middle of Bourbon

Street, bodies oblivious to her and to the reason she is now among them.

She presses on, tacking through the dense currents, following any little opening in the general direction of the bar for as far as possible and then shifting into the next opening, and in this way she is making progress, and the chanting and cheering is fading into the distance behind her. And for all the intense and indiscriminate jostling of a Mardi Gras middle-of-the-street crowd, it's rare that anyone there will consciously put a hand on a stranger, so she's doing better now, she's even able to convince herself she's had an adventure at Mardi Gras, she's got a good story to tell.

And she finds herself seated on the side of the bed in the Olivier House and it's twenty-five years later and she thinks: I'm telling the story to myself now. And she wonders why. She should have a drink. But instead, here's this story playing itself out. Michael is about to appear for the first time. That's the prompt. Meeting him, of course, has ultimately led to this present moment. But her mind has backed her up farther than necessary to introduce her future husband, and it occurs to her the reason is this: the bag is Gucci, the dress is Chanel; I've shown my tits. But that feels wrong, somehow. Too simple. The two librarians wanted to be desired. But at the moment they lifted their tops to show their naked breasts, weren't their yearnings running deeper than that? And she stops this thinking. Stops it.

Michael still insists on presenting himself, however. Kelly emerges at last from that Bourbon Street crowd and she goes into the bar on the corner of Toulouse, and there she learns yet another thing about Mardi Gras: you don't split up and expect to find each other again. Kelly makes a thorough tour of the frat and sorority drunks, and a Yoda drinking with a Ken and Barbie, and the Blues Brothers in a corner table—half a dozen of them—singing the chorus of "Rubber Biscuit," and the dazed and queasy women in the toilet at the back. But Katie and Theresa are gone.

Kelly doesn't want to drink alone. She's had enough close encounters with strangers. The three of them have an arranged meeting place if they get split up anyway, back at their hotel room across Canal Street. She steps out of the bar, and with the tumult on Bourbon and with Toulouse Street to her right that, by comparison, is only thinly and casually populated, she strolls off toward Rampart.

But almost at once a loud, slurred meowing begins behind her.

She knows not to stop, not even to look. But she takes only a few more steps and on each side of

her a body rushes by and the two converge before
her to block her way, and she stops. The two young
men look faintly familiar in a fleetingly-witnessed-
crime-and-now-pick-them-out-of-a-lineup sort
of way. She remembers. They are the drunks who
meowed at her earlier. Not frat-boyish really. Spiky
hair and bad teeth. Townies somewhere. Grease mon-
keys and 7-Eleven clerks. They are blondish and could
be brothers. They are holding drinks in Styrofoam
cups and they are draped in beads. The taller, heavier,
older of the two shifts his eyes briefly over Kelly's
shoulder. She remembers there was a third and she
knows he's behind her. And there is a clutching in
her throat as palpable as if one of them has grabbed
her there with his hand.

The taller of the two says, "The cat. The cat's back."

The smaller says, "Catwoman. Cat girl."

Kelly takes a single tentative, sliding step to the
left and the two men shift with her.

"Whoa," the older one says. "You're all dressed
up for us."

"Looking good," the other says.

In a low, calm way the older one says, "Show
your tits."

His little brother struggles to take a cheap strand
of beads from the tangle on his neck. The older brother

looks Kelly steadily in the eyes. "Show your tits," he says again.

The other one stops struggling with the beads and says, "Tits. Can you show us six? Do cats have six?"

"Two," the older one says. "It's Cat*woman*."

"Two's better."

"Show us." This comes from behind Kelly. The third man.

"Show your tits," they all three say. And they begin to chant it. "Show your tits. Show your tits."

The chanting seems less a threat than the older one's quiet demand and Kelly takes another step to the side and even as she thinks to run, her legs wobble, her knees won't hold firmly, her ankle turns a little in the stilettos. And the third man appears, a dark-haired one, stocky, and the three shoulder up and the older blondish one, still the leader, says "Tits first" and Kelly makes a little movement to the side again but the three of them together are quick, they shift too, keeping in front of her and she's having trouble drawing a breath and the three of them don't chant this time but say in low, intense unison, "Show your tits."

Then an arm is around her waist and a man's voice says "The cat's with me" and the arm is strong and presses her gently but firmly to move. Instantly the leader of the men takes a step toward them saying

"Who's this asshole . . ." and the man holding Kelly blocks the other man with a carefully modulated stiff arm, not quite touching him but firmly placed between them, meaning serious business but not quite aggressive enough to start a fight, not yet at least, and he says in an elaborately friendly tone "Chill out, man" and this is all going very fast for Kelly and she is trying to catch up and she has not even looked at this new man, and she does that now. She sees Michael's profile for the first time, the sweet hard prominence of chin and brow, and at this moment she doesn't know who he is or, in fact, if his intentions are any better than the others'. But she can sort that out later. She shifts closer into him and he's saying to the leader of the three, in that friendly tone, "It's all just a great party here."

Michael again gently presses her to move and they do, together, taking a step up Toulouse, but the stocky one lurches in front of them, blocking the way, and the man says, "Hey, this is between us and her." Michael's arm slides from around Kelly's waist and he gently elbows her away from him. She complies. She takes a few steps, goes up onto the sidewalk, but she does not keep going, as Michael perhaps wishes for her to do. She turns and watches.

Michael too has shifted a step away, but not in retreat. He squares up to confront all three at once, not just the dark one who blocked their retreat. "Gentle-men," he says, "there are plenty of easy tits around the corner. You don't want to do it the hard way in this town. You'll spill your beer."

And now everything comes to a stop. Michael and the three men stare at each other in silence, not moving. The drunks are weighing as best they can the risks and the gains. The only movement is the smaller blond looking briefly down at the cup in his hand, apparently to ponder the spilling of his beer. Michael is wide in the shoulders. Michael has thick upper arms. Michael is utterly motionless and Kelly cannot see his face, but ten years later she will watch him from behind in a courtroom at a murder trial and she will not see his face but he will be staring down a cop he suspects faked some evidence and she will think that his face is the same as it was on the first day they met.

The silence between the four men persists. In real-ity it is probably not more than a few seconds, but it's a long time, a very long time, for Kelly. As an observer she is free to begin to flush hot and grow limb-restless with fear for herself and for this man trying to help her. And she knows the situation needs some new element, something Michael did not presume to add himself, either from macho simplicity or from deference to her. But she can do this.

"Darling," she says. "Will you promise never to leave me alone again at Mardi Gras? I don't care how bad you have to piss."

The three drunken men glance to her: if the asshole who's messing with their game isn't just a stranger trying to be a hero, if in fact he's really with the bitch, then the situation changes somewhat. Not necessarily a lot—this is a guy thing now, with its own life—but enough that Michael recognizes a brief opportunity. He turns his back on the men and takes a step toward Kelly.

"Just stay where I put you next time," he says.

She takes a step toward him and there is a rush in her from its being time to try to walk away. And from the man's face. She is seeing Michael's face straight on for the first time. His eyes are dark and heavy-lidded and steady on her and the rush in her may be mostly about his face, even the walking away part is about his eyes now. His arm is around her again and they take a step together up Toulouse and another, and now that he's holding her she finds she's starting to let go to what's been happening and the trembling is beginning, she might well tremble already at his touch, but this is mostly about what's been happening with these other men and she is wobbly in the legs once more.

Michael says, low, "Let's move a little briskly."

And they do. They push on faster. No cries or curses follow them. Surely macho-crazed drunks in pursuit would make a loud show of it. And even with the din of Mardi Gras coming from Bourbon Street, she does hear their own feet brisking on the pavement, carrying them away.

Michael brings his face close to hers. "That was smart, what you said."

Kelly wants to reply, but the farther they get from the danger, the more she realizes this incident is over, the more she trembles, and she can't quite shape any words. And this man—Michael, the man she will marry a little over a year later—this man seems to her to understand everything.

"Look," he says. "I'm staying in a hotel up ahead. Would you like to go there and collect yourself? If you prefer, I can just put you in the room and disappear."

And Kelly finds her voice. "Thanks," she says. "Yes. But don't disappear."

~

On one side of the four-poster rice bed lies Laurie's hoop-skirted gown in white watered silk and trimmed in crimson pleated satin. On the other side of the bed, propped up against the backboard, is Michael, still dressed in the black jeans and polo shirt he wore for the drive. He has just put his cell phone into its holster and laid it on the night table: no message from his lawyer that the morning hearing, the finalizing of the divorce, is done with. Not that he needs an instant report. Max knows Michael wants to just get away from all that. Max can handle it. Michael plays that little litany a bit more: It's what a lawyer is for, especially a lawyer's lawyer. Let this thing go.

And Laurie emerges from the bathroom, damp and wrapped in a towel knotted at the center of her chest. She stands at the foot of the bed and Michael looks at her and she looks back at him. This goes on for a few seconds, and Laurie wonders if Michael needs to be a movie star to be fully understood: where his face is ten feet high, maybe the nothing that is so often there would actually become a nuanced something.

She smiles the faintest of smiles at him. "So if I put my hand here," she says, putting her hand on the knot of the towel, "would you sit up straight and widen your eyes and start breathing heavy?"

"Of course," Michael says.

She waits. Her hand is still there. He is not moving. His face is not changing.

"Well?" she says.

Michael makes a minute movement of his head, a slight tilt and release and return to his previous uprightness. A movie-actor-sized shrug. "That's just the hypothetical demonstration," he says.

"You are a funny bunny," Laurie says. "John Wayne by way of Clarence Darrow by way of Mount Rushmore."

"Drop your towel, my dear. I won't disappoint you. But you were anxious to turn into Scarlett, and the night is long."

"You're right, darling. This should wait. We'll make it a real occasion." She turns her back to him and takes a step toward the bathroom, saying, "You're not ready." She tosses this over her shoulder but with an admonitory firmness.

"I'm fast," he says.

"I hope you're talking about getting dressed," she says, and without looking back at him, she whips off her towel. She hasn't yet fully figured out her handsomely ripening Michael Hays, Esquire, but be that as it may, the sight of her perfect ass seems a relevant point to make at the moment.

And with the sudden showing of the long, sweet nakedness of the back of her body, Michael's breath catches, and then, as the bathroom door clicks shut, an afterimage blooms and clarifies into flesh and his breath catches again at the sight of Kelly, in his room at the Olivier House the morning after their first Mardi Gras: she has risen and she is moving away from the bed and she ripples through him, the long, sweet nakedness of her, down the indent of her spine to the sweet fullness of her backside cleavage, and she vanishes around the corner of the wall on her way to the bathroom. Michael is left propped on pillows against the wrought iron headboard, and he turns his face to the open French windows and to the striking silence there, the silence of Ash Wednesday, the silence after the clamorous rush of Fat Tuesday, like the silence after sex.

He rests for a time in both those silences, and then he hears the soft whisk of Kelly's approach, and she is beside him again and her arm slides over his chest and the long length of her leg falls gently upon his and her head comes to rest against his shoulder. He slips his arm around her back and lays his hand on the point of her hip and presses her close. But he keeps his eyes on the dove-gray sky out the windows.

And they lie like this for a while, until Kelly says, "You're a quiet man."

"Am I?" Michael thinks about it. He has already spoken to her of his work in the firm. And of Pensacola and Florida politics and even, a bit, of the fishing in the Gulf. "I think I talk a lot," he says.

"When you make love you're quiet," she says. "I hope I didn't embarrass you."

"You scream charmingly," he says.

"I should give it up for Lent."

"Can you?"

"Just the screaming," Kelly says.

He smiles out the windows at this. Then he initiates a shifting of their bodies to lie facing each other, the official small-talk going-on-with-things after having made love for the first time.

He ripples again, from her eyes: they are large and they are as dark as the Gulf in the night and they are wide with the newness of their intimacy. On her forehead is a thumbed cross of ashes.

He lifts his hand and gently draws a fingertip across the ashes. "You went out early."

"Did I wake you?"

"Are you Catholic?"

"No," she says. "It's just a remembrance. That we all die."

"Today only in the Elizabethan sense," he says.

"That's why I'll never give up sex for Lent," she says. "It's already the little death."

"And that's why I'm quiet when we do it," Michael says.

Kelly smiles and she puts a hand in the center of his chest and she pushes him flat and she glides over him and rises above him and she bends to kiss him.

Michael sits up abruptly in his cottage at Oak Alley and he swings his legs off the bed. He does this to stop the memory. He sits there, a little hunched, and he tries to think about putting on a damned-fool of an antebellum swallow-tail dress coat, but he is still kissing Kelly on Ash Wednesday morning, 1984.

~

And Kelly has, in the flow of her own memory, moved to the same Ash Wednesday morning, and she is screaming as something trembles into focus, into startled clarity inside her, trembles in the place where their bodies are joined and trembles outward into her limbs, her fingertips, her toes. And the silence of this man, which she has noticed at the back of her mind, deepens now even as she forgets about his silence and everything else, and her eyes are squeezed shut. So her memory does not contain—nor does her understanding of this man account for—the fact that his eyes are open and holding steady on her as his body clarifies itself in its own rushing heartbeat of a way.

And she will never realize—in all the times of love-making in the quarter of a century before them—that he always keeps his eyes only on her face when his moment begins.

As for Kelly sitting on the side of the bed twenty-five years later, her memory has dissolved into the quiet time after they first made love. They are entwined on the bed and Michael turns his face to her and his fingertip is tracking across her forehead.

"You got up early," he says.

She understands what his fingertip has found. She lifts her own hand, takes his, brings that fingertip to her mouth and kisses it, finishing the kiss, on an impulse, by parting her lips and touching the ash there with her tongue, which yields a faint texture but no taste. Death should have a strong taste, should burn on the tongue. This is too easy.

"So you're Catholic?" Michael says.

"Did I wake you?" she says.

He shakes his head no.

"I'm not Catholic," she says. "I just do the ashes as a remembrance. We all die."

"Today only in the Elizabethan sense," he says.

"Now that's a good reason not to give up sex for Lent. The little death."

She thinks she sees a tiny pop of his eyebrows at this. He didn't expect her to get the joke. She sings softly, "There's always something there to remind me."

He doesn't laugh or even smile. He looks at her steadily. But surely in that steadiness is affection. Even if her little outburst of song didn't charm him into a smile, this steadiness has to be good. And she makes a mistake. As unthinkingly as touching her tongue to the ashes, she says, "Are you glad we met?"

She regrets it at once. His face does not change. Not a flicker of difference. This came out of nowhere for him, she realizes. But his face doesn't even show surprise. That's a good sign surely. But there is this scrabbling of need that's come upon her. "Yes?" she asks.

And as tiny as the pop of his eyebrows a few moments ago, there is a brief, quick lift of the corners of his mouth. A minute smile. "You know the answer to that," he says.

This is way short of what she needs at the moment. But they made love. He saved her and was gentle with her afterwards, not taking advantage of her vulnerability, not pushing for sex, ready to vanish from his own rooms if she wished and then from her life, but she asked him to stay and he held her and they made love—beginning with the same impulse in both of them at the same moment—impossible even to say who started it—and he thinks her screams are charming when she comes—he said this just a few moments ago, when she was feeling embarrassed. So all this is enough. For now. This is enough.

And in the present, Kelly abruptly rises from the side of the bed. She wants to shout something across the years, some denial to her stupid young self, wants to shout that aloud now. But she doesn't. She struggles to stay silent, to stand perfectly still, and she succeeds. Of course she does. She's not crazy.

~

Michael has not moved from the side of the bed as Laurie hums in the bathroom. He has stopped kissing Kelly on the Ash Wednesday morning when all that would happen between them truly began. He should start dressing for Laurie, but he is putting on a tuxedo now for Kelly. He steps from the master bedroom cedar closet in their Craftsman house on the Bayou Texar. They've moved in at last. The muted pitch to its gabled roof, the exposed but rounded and polished rafters, the redwood shingles: all this feels like him and he appreciates that Kelly has let the house be him in these things, without his having to persuade her. She is presently campaigning for an Arkansas governor trying to be president who hasn't got a rat's-ass chance of the nomination, and later in the evening Michael will watch as Bill Clinton shakes Kelly's hand with both his and he will watch how Clinton continues to hold that handshake for the longest time, even as the two of them talk on, and Michael will see her looking up into this man's eyes and on the night when the man wins she will be curled up on their couch with Michael and she will weep and sing along: *Don't stop thinking about tomorrow.* But now Michael steps out of the closet and he hates wearing this tuxedo and she knows it but he's doing it for her—he simply pressed his lips tight together when she asked and he saw her eyes go to his lips and he knew she was seeing his feelings there and he knew she knew how he hates dressing up formally but how he'll do it for her—and now he steps from the closet and she comes to him and looks up into his eyes and she holds his gaze for a moment, smiling faintly, and she straightens his tie. "Thank you," she says. And no more needs to be said, and he is content. He thinks this is a moment when it is all good. As good as it can be between a man and a woman. He has quietly done this simple domestic thing on her behalf. She says two words to acknowledge that. They look at each other.

His tie is straight, though such a thing isn't important to him and even makes him oddly uncomfortable and she knows it and her little smile says to him she's all right with his not caring about his tie but he will let it stay straight tonight for her, he'll even stop before the mirror before he leaves the restroom at the fundraiser and he'll straighten it himself, on her behalf. And he is not jealous of her joy at shaking Bill Clinton's hand or of the man holding on too goddam long. He trusts Kelly. He trusts her instinctively and completely.

And he stops his mind now, as Laurie's hair dryer roars on the other side of the bathroom door. He stops and he is about to rise and dress in a suit of clothes even more alien to him than that tuxedo. And along the way in this memory he's just had—in his lingering for just a moment over the contentment he felt in the two of them wordlessly understanding each other—an even earlier event coursed beneath the surface. Michael does not go there now. He couldn't even consciously summon this deeper memory if he was moved to try. But his sense of ease with Kelly on the night of the Clinton fundraiser was rooted in that past event, for it had given him an initial impression of what his life would be with Kelly, and that impression settled into him, and it would not change for a quarter of a century. The impression would remain and affect everything,

even though the memory of the event itself would
eventually vanish.

It was this: Later on that same Ash Wednesday
morning of their first days together, they have been
walking the quiet Quarter and there have been some
lovely moments between them and some awkward
moments between them and Michael doesn't know
what to do about this woman and they find their way
to the Café du Monde. They sit at street's edge in the
café's open-air pavilion and order beignets and chicory
coffee and the waiter moves off, and Michael and Kelly
sit across from each other at the tiny bistro table, and
he is afraid there will be talk, earnest talk. But instead,
they look each other in the eyes and she doesn't ask
him to speak, she doesn't seem to wish to talk at all.
They look each other in the eyes and they don't look
away and this goes on for a few moments and a few
moments more and her face is not compressed into
questions, not restless, her face is not seeking something,
her face is placid, an unrippled pond bright from daylight but without even a reflection there, and Michael
untenses, unlocks, he feels his own face go calm, and
he and Kelly don't look away from each other. And this
goes on. They look at each other steadily for a long
while and then somewhere about her eyes she shows
the tiniest moon-ascension increment of a threshold

smile, but it too holds and persists without pushing on and he does not have to deal with it, does not have to smile as well or be forced not to smile in return, it is a simple thing with no demands on him, and his chest and arms and shoulders go quiet, his mind goes quiet, he knows he can be good with this woman and she can be good with him. And as they look each other silently in the eyes just like this for a long while more, this impression of Kelly burrows deeply into Michael, and the memory of this moment will vanish from his conscious memory and only the impression itself will remain. And so, as Michael sits on the side of the bed now, asserting his characteristic control over his mind, backing away from the past, thinking to put on an antebellum tuxedo and missing the irony of that, he does not overtly remember those few minutes when there was only silence and hope and the sudden inevitability of the future between him and the woman who, he assumes, ceased being his wife this morning.

~

Michael stands inside the front door of the cottage, dressed for Laurie, his hands clasped behind his back, thinking to step outside to wait but hesitating as he deals with a niggling unease at showing himself in public in costume. He finished dressing while Laurie was still knocking around in the bathroom and he has a faint moue of a thought about how his wife—his ex-wife now, surely, given that declining sun before him—how his ex-wife and this woman from an entirely different generation share in some sort of ancient female gene which makes them compulsively and needlessly worry that their men won't get dressed in time. And now, this glancing off of Kelly, even vaguely, even over some little quotidian quirk—how she always fussed at him to hurry up, hurry up and get ready—this murmur of Kelly in him makes his hands unclasp and drop to his sides for a moment and then bury themselves in his pants pockets. And he shuts down his mind on this whole subject. He can't let himself think about Kelly.

"So." This is Laurie's voice, behind him. She speaks just the one word. A verbalized clearing of the throat. Michael takes his hands from his pockets, and he turns to face her. Laurie is framed in the doorway from the dining room. She is wearing her white silk hoop-skirted gown and her shoulders are bare and she has her hands demurely clasped before her at the waist. She smiles a small-scale, self-satisfied smile, and her hands separate and float out beside her, and as they do, her smile expands, calibrates itself for a multitude. She steps into the room and does a slow, elegant twirl.

And Michael is standing in the central reception hall
in his house, and behind him he hears the rustle of his
daughter's expected descent from the second floor. She
makes a sound to let him know she is there. Perhaps
even a single, simple word: So. He turns. Samantha is
seventeen and she is going to the prom. She poses near
the bottom of the staircase, her hands clasped before
her at the waist. Her shoulders are bare. They shouldn't
be bare, he thinks, though when she swims, they are
bare—at the pool far more of his teenage daughter
is also bare—and he has come to accept that, but he
can't help thinking her shoulders shouldn't be bare in
a dress like this, worn for a seventeen-year-old boy
as dumbshittedly hormonal as the boy who is soon
to arrive, and Michael knows that he has to let all
this go, that inside his head—even in there, where he
should know how to be reasonable and controlled—
he is being a foolish cliché of a father. What does not
occur to him is that he should be saying something
to Sam now about how beautiful she looks. He stands
looking at her and the standing part becomes a bit
unsteady, for her beauty actually staggers him. But
he does not know how to put that into words—does
not have the emotional mechanism to put that into
words—so he shoves his hands into his pockets. Sam
waits and then she steps forward and she twirls for

him, slowly. Kelly arrives from the back of the house. "Sam!" she cries. "You're so beautiful!" And though Kelly is also in the room, Sam ends her twirl facing Michael. "You'll be the Queen of the Prom!" Kelly cries. Sam waits for her father. He pulls his hands out of his pockets and he tilts his head slightly to the side and he is certain he is smiling his approval, he feels certain that he is smiling and that smiling is enough. Sam steps closer to him and he opens his arms and she presses against him and he hugs her. And this is more than enough. He is proud of himself for not saying anything about her shoulders. And Sam lets go of him and moves off to her mother and wordful hugs, and he does not realize he has disappointed her—he has no idea whatsoever—and she does not know how to ask for what she needs from him and so she does not understand that her beauty has truly registered on him, registered so powerfully, indeed, that six years later, in the presence of this other young beautiful woman, he is spontaneously filled with a vision of his daughter's beauty even though that is the last thing he wants in his head right now, a reminder that the woman he will have sex with in a few hours is—as he expects will be murmured about in a room full of strangers tonight—young enough to be his daughter.

"Is the jury still out?" Laurie says.

Michael doesn't understand. "What?"

"The verdict, counselor. I'm awaiting the verdict." Laurie's voice is keeping it light, but she is realizing she has some work to do with this man, and if she hadn't just dressed herself up and if he weren't looking so soothingly sturdily handsomely fine in his high collar and white marcella tie, she'd start right now. Some loosening spade work. But his reticent stiffness still has a certain charm for her, and it certainly feels antebellum, so she waits for a long moment with her smile turned indulgent and then says, "Am I stunningly beautiful?"

The question actually surprises Michael. His first thought is: you know damn well you are. But he knows not to say that. "Yes," he does say, and if he had his way, that would be sufficient. But he can see her wanting more, and he says, "Of that you're guilty beyond any reasonable doubt."

Laurie laughs. "Cheers in the courtroom," she says.

And Michael thinks he has said and done the right thing. With Laurie. With Sam. With Laurie and with Sam. And with Kelly? He won't touch that. He wants to call Max. He wants just to call Max and have him say two words: It's done. Come on, Max. He probably went straight to court afterwards for some other case. But what the hell is text messaging for? Michael's cell phone is secreted beneath his swallowtail coat, but not asking about Kelly is part of the letting go of her. He'll wait it out for now.

"Let's promenade," Laurie says, and she's beside him, she's turning him, she's slipping her hand into the crook of his arm.

~

Kelly has been standing beside the bed for a long while. She has turned her head and she has been staring at the bottle of Scotch. The Scotch primarily, but for a time, of course, the bottle of pills registered on her as well, out of focus, away from the center of the picture of the night table she composed for herself when she first turned her head. But now just the Scotch. The Scotch still sealed and dim in the shadow on the other side of this great swath of sunlight pouring through the French windows onto the bed. The Scotch keeps her mind quiet. No memories at all, really. Just the bottle. Just the look of it there. Just its being there. But eventually it lets this in: a bottle of Scotch still sealed sitting in the center of the long, mahogany dining room table and her sitting at a right angle to it, turning her head to look at it and then turning away, looking straight before her along the table to the window and the water oaks outside and the bayou. An egret passes before her, beats its wings once in the slow, massive way of the egrets, as slow and vast as she herself could feel if she were to drink this Scotch. And Kelly's chest clamps shut with a sound. A phone ringing. Muffled, though. Her chest releases. But the puzzlement remains. And her hand moves to the sound and she finds her cell phone in a pocket of the terrycloth robe that she is also surprised about, to find she's wearing a robe. But yes. She showered. She put this on. She came down the steps. She took her cell phone from her purse. She thought to drink awhile. She got the bottle. She put the bottle on the dining room table. She sat beside it. She made a call. And the phone is still ringing and she takes it from her pocket and the screen says "Sam."

She opens the phone and puts it to her ear.

"Mama," Sam's voice says.

"Hey, Sam." This is her own voice.

"I'm sorry I didn't hear my phone ring," Sam says.

"Where are you, baby?"

"Chicago, Mama. I've got a gig tomorrow."

"I'm very proud of you."

"What's going on, Mama?"

"Other than the obvious?" Kelly says this even as she refuses to let her mind turn overtly to that obvious thing. She does not let it in. Either as she speaks to her daughter or as she presently stands beside the bed.

"Your message," Sam says.

"What did I say, baby?"

"You were wet. You were dry. You wondered why you'd never fully appreciated Scotch before."

"All true."

"You don't remember the message?"

"Of course I do," Kelly says, and she hears herself laugh. But she has remembered the message only after Sam told her. And she wonders: have I already been drinking today? But she knows she hasn't. She even knows now, standing by the bed, that the bottle of Scotch on the dining table with Sam on the phone and a pale, thin-clouded sunlight out the window is the same bottle of Scotch she has brought to Room 303.

Kelly turns her face from the night table. Why has she waited this long to open that bottle? She's never had any trouble opening a bottle. It's never been her first or her obsessive impulse to open a bottle—even since this all began, since the ending of her and Michael—but she can readily do it and she was certainly ready yesterday to open the bottle and she didn't. And she shudders, deep in the center of her chest, she shudders and then faintly quakes on, because she knows the other bottle near her now, the other bottle on the night stand, is why the seal on the Scotch hasn't been broken. Yesterday it wasn't yet about this other bottle. She knows the plan is larger now. No. There is no plan. There are just more possibilities.

She moves away, finds herself before a flower-print wingback chair in the corner beyond the French windows. She sits. The bottle, the bed, the sunlight across the room are distant now. But Samantha is still close. Kelly tries to force herself back in time. She flails for something of Sam that hasn't to do with the mess. Some good thing. Some good moment. But she cannot will this. She has to wait for whatever is next.

~

In the quarter-mile brick allée between the highway and the Big House, two dozen couples swan about beneath the canopy of live oaks. Actually a brace of swans and one coot, Michael thinks. But he makes sure his arm is always available for Laurie's hand. And for her sake, he returns every smile, careful to give no sign that he is uncomfortable in this get-up. He feels Laurie's animation next to him as he nods with her at a passing couple, her hand squeezing at his bicep. He puts his hand over hers on his arm. He pats her. He's happy she's happy. And he keeps his bicep tensed on her account, aware of this little outburst of vanity, trying to show off a muscle. He blinks a slow blink of self-criticism but keeps the muscle flexed.

When the most recent couple is out of earshot, Laurie says, low, "What's she thinking of, with those leg-of-mutton sleeves?"

"Dinner?" Michael says.

With her free hand Laurie knuckle-frogs him on the arm. "Queen fricking Victoria is the answer," she says.

"Man. You're as good at that as Sammy Bunker."

"Tell me he's a costume expert."

"Frogging expert. I had a perpetual shoulder bruise in fifth grade."

She hits him again. And she really is good at this. After the second stroke, she instantly looks away, studying the other dresses ahead on the allée. The throb of pain from her knuckle and her instant obliviousness to the assault charms Michael.

They are approaching the slate-floored terrace and front veranda of the house, the path passing through clusters of round, white-clothed tables set with candles and china for the dinner tonight. Laurie guides them in a U-turn to head back down the allée. At the far end, across Highway 18, is the berm of the levee, and seeing it now lets Michael pick up a sound from beyond, the grumble of a push boat out on the river moving barges of rice or fertilizer or asphalt up the Mississippi. He's glad to put his mind out there, out of sight of the house and the playacting, but he feels Laurie squeeze at his arm and straighten and slow down their pace.

He focuses before him and a couple is approaching. Young. Laurie's age or so. The woman is pretty and her shoulders are bony; the man is carefully coiffed, expensively so, almost certainly, and Michael has a hunch about him. The two couples stop before each other.

"You look wonderful," Laurie says to the woman.

"So do you," the woman says.

"I'm Laurie Pruitt. This is Michael Hays."

They all start shaking hands and the others are saying their names—Jason Murray and Madison Murray—and Jason's handshake has a certain glad, inquisitive aggressiveness to it, which supports Michael's initial hunch.

"This is my first of these," Laurie says. "How about you?"

"Our fourth," Jason answers, though Laurie was looking at Madison when she asked the question.

"We were married here," Madison says. "At this event."

"Oh that's so cool," Laurie says.

Now Jason and Madison turn their faces in unison to Michael, awaiting his declaration. Laurie looks at Michael and he's not answering instantly and she is prepared to answer for him. But even as she is beginning to shape the first word in her mouth, Michael lifts his shoulders in a slightly exaggerated shrug. "I'm a codger lawyer with a young girlfriend who looks great in ruffles and is ardent to wear them."

The three young faces before Michael freeze, very briefly, as certain witnesses sometimes freeze for him in rare and wonderful moments in a courtroom. But then these three brighten abruptly and laugh.

"I'm a lawyer, too," Jason says. "Baton Rouge."

Michael has already guessed the lawyer part.

"We're from Pensacola," Laurie says.

"Personal injury?" Michael says.

Jason is caught off guard yet again, though he instantly masks it. "Yes," he says. "Does it show?"

"The handshake," Michael says.

"Really." Jason inflects this as a statement, not a question.

Michael means all this in a collegial, insider sort of way, but he can hear a professional prickle beginning in Jason.

"You do look great in ruffles," Madison says to Laurie.

"So do you," Laurie says.

"You must be a D.A.," Jason says, tainting this with a scorn clear enough to be audible to another lawyer but light enough that he could believably deny it to a non-lawyer if challenged.

Michael has eaten youngsters like this alive in courtrooms. He does one of his small, fine-tuned, faux self-deprecating shrugs. "Nah," he says. "I'm just a Swiss Army knife of a lawyer. Whatever you need."

"Personal injury?" Jason cocks his head.

"I leave that to the experts," Michael says. And after a tiny pause, he adds, "So if I ever botch a divorce and get plugged by an unhappy husband and don't die, I'll give you a call."

"Or by an unhappy wife," Jason says, and he does not look at Laurie. His restraint, even as he counter-punches, makes Michael smile a small, approving smile at the young man.

"Sir," Michael says, drawing the word out, "would gentlemen in suits like ours actually sue a woman?"

Jason smiles a small smile in return.

"We'll see you both at the ball?" Laurie says.

"Oh yes," Madison says.

The two men nod at each other.

"Sir," Jason says.

"Sir," Michael says, crooking his arm for Laurie but keeping his eyes on his fellow lawyer.

Laurie slips her hand into its place on Michael's flexed bicep, and they move away. They walk for a few moments in the direction of the distant levee and Laurie says, low, "Whenever your sort meets, do you always start pissing on the same tree?"

"It's our upbringing," Michael says. "We are who we are."

~

And Kelly sits in the flower-print wingback chair in the corner, in the shadows, and she has once more returned to the beginning of things, to the time when she met Michael, when she first loved him. After they make love on Ash Wednesday morning, after her mistake of asking for a declaration from him, they fall into silence; she lets this quiet man set the mood. He does slide his arm around her, though he turns his face away, toward the open French windows. But he draws her close and they remain silent for a long while, and then they face the fact they will have to check out of the hotel in a couple of hours and it's hard even to say who makes the first movement but one or the other of them does and they rise together without any further words and they dress and they go out.

They stroll down Toulouse and turn on Chartres and approach the flagstone mall between the cast-iron-fenced Jackson Square and the St. Louis Cathedral. She has slipped her hand into the crook of his arm. She can feel the rock-hardness of his bicep and it assures her, somehow, the body taking on the metaphor for the man himself. Solid. And from that, dependable. He can keep her safe, happy. His arm moves them forward. The mall is nearly deserted. No drunks. Only a few people passing through with faces lowered. Only a stray Mardi Gras doubloon or a broken length of beads swept tight against the curb.

As Michael and Kelly cross in front of the Cathedral, the bell begins to toll above them, the deep prelude and then the solemnly paced counting, heading, at this moment, up to ten. Kelly slows at the sound, and Michael follows her lead now. She stops them. She looks up the center of the three, slate-cloaked spires. "Can you wait a little for your coffee?" she asks. She knows the morning will soon end, the two of them will part. But the bell tolled a reminder as she passed, so she will sit here beneath it for a while, trying to hold on to time.

"I can wait," he says.

They sit on an iron bench, behind them the Square and Andy Jackson rearing high on his horse, before them the Cathedral. Kelly puts her head on Michael's shoulder and she closes her eyes to rest in this present moment without a thought to the next, but as soon as she does, a feeling tremors through her like the vibration of the Cathedral bell. She lifts her head and opens her eyes. She needed something from him in the room. Seeking it did not turn out well. But now she has no choice.

"It all ends so abruptly," she says, keeping her eyes forward, not looking at Michael.

He is silent.

"And completely," she says. Now she turns her head to him. He is looking about the mall.

He nods at the cathedral. "That's why they tolerate it," he says. "They get you back today, big time. And you need them more than ever."

Kelly has begun this and she will not retreat. But she resists saying it directly: this time together is ending so abruptly, whatever it is that's between us also will end. She puts it on him: "You think I was talking about Mardi Gras?"

He looks at her. But his face shows nothing. She has no idea what he's feeling. And she grows afraid. She's a fool to push this now. So she takes the burden off him to speak—even to feel—and she curses her own cowardice as she forces a sweet smile and says, "You're right. I was."

He looks at her—as if blankly—for a moment and then he says, "The next logical question . . . But why don't I know this yet?" And there is a leaping in her: she knows what he's referring to. He's not blank at all. He understands what she's feeling. In spite of his seeming blankness.

"Where I live," she says.

"Yes," Michael says.

Sitting now on the flower-print chair with the two bottles on the night table across the room, Kelly stops the memory for a moment. Her eyes grow tight with unreleased tears. She is struck by this: how abiding and deep an early impression we can draw of another person from a single, unexamined incident. That he did know what she was talking about. That he was himself feeling what she was feeling. The tears express themselves now and she does not touch them. Did she trust this early impression too much or not enough over the years to come? As strongly as she wanted to be in the fullness of present-time on that Ash Wednesday, she cannot be in this moment now, this present, this circumstance. She lets Ash Wednesday play on.

"We skipped some stages, didn't we," Kelly says to Michael as they sit on the iron bench before the Cathedral.

"We did," he says.

"Mobile," she says.

He smiles. "A 'Bama girl."

"Big-city 'Bama."

"Oh it shows," Michael says.

And now his blankness is a comic's deadpan. It's all okay, she thinks, as she laughs. "And you?" she says.

"Florida, then and now. We neither of us fell far from the tree."

"Were you barefoot and chewing grass in a town with two blinking lights?"

"Pretty close," he says.

"It shows," she says, keeping her own face straight.

He doesn't laugh. Kelly—a little to her surprise—does not worry about his being offended. She isn't picking up any of that. She senses him thinking about his small-town Florida, but simply serious thoughts, perhaps nostalgic ones.

She's wrong. He says, "You mentioned something about your sister."

She feels that little leaping again. She realizes instantly that he has come back to a consideration of the end of their time together. "She's long gone," Kelly says.

"Do you have a plan?"

"Please," she says, in two, long, are-you-kidding-me syllables.

Michael smiles at this and then sets his face again. "I can drop you," he says.

This takes Kelly by surprise. "Really?"

"I've got shoes and cycling traffic lights in my present Florida town. Pensacola. You're right on the way."

"So it's not over?" Kelly says. "Not abruptly at least?"

Michael rises, stands over her, offers his hand. "Coffee first," he says. "With chicory."

And they sit nursing the New Orleans chicory-root coffee under the open-air pavilion of the Café du Monde. And Kelly lifts a beignet, extending her ring and little fingers, trying to be 'Bamagirl-dainty, but though its square, doughnutty texture is manageable, when she brings the beignet to her mouth, the coating of powdered sugar suddenly, profusely pollinates her face from her mistimed downward breath.

Michael sharply leans to her and speaks with urgency. "Don't breathe back in. It'll coat your lungs."

This makes her laugh and the laugh jostles her beignet, which releases another cloud of sugar.

"Don't laugh," Michael says. "It can be fatal."

She puts the beignet down on her plate. "We'll just look at them," she says.

And she begins to do just that, laying her hands on the tabletop and lowering her face and staring at the three beignets sitting in a snow drift of sugar on the plate. She does this for several moments, playing out the joke, but she can dimly see in the upper periphery of her downward sight that Michael does not move, he remains fixed on her.

Kelly lifts her face to him. And she and Michael begin wordlessly to look each other in the eyes for a long, long while, though as Kelly sits in the flower-print chair in Room 303 on the day she has failed to finish her divorce, she does not remember that the silence was extended. This was the unexamined incident that gave Michael his deep and abiding early impression of what life would be with Kelly. For Michael, the influential part was the silence, even as the incidence of that silence has now faded from his conscious memory. Of how he ended the silence, he has no memory whatsoever, conscious or unconscious, though it is this final gesture that makes Kelly squeeze hard with both hands at the arms of her chair beside the French windows.

Michael's eyes shift ever so slightly upward, and Kelly realizes he is looking at the cross of ashes still on her forehead. And now he looks down at the beignets before him, and he puts the tip of his forefinger into the powdered sugar at the margin of his plate, and he lifts his finger, coated white, and he reaches out, across the table, and he touches Kelly's forehead, touches the dark cross of ashes, and he traces a white cross of sugar there.

And he says, "In remembrance of life. And to a thing not ended."

~

Kelly's hands on the arms of the chair eventually loosen their grip. They rub there for a while, even as her mind shuts down. She rubs there and rubs there and then her hands finally stop. How long has she been sitting here utterly empty? The sun is still on the bed. Perhaps not so very long. How unbearably sweetly it all began, yes? Very sweetly. The cross of sugar. Sugar Wednesday. No, Kelly thinks. "Remember you are dust and unto dust you will return." Did she say that aloud just now? Perhaps. She and Michael are walking along the Gulf shore, the barrier island just south of Pensacola. The sand is fine and white and the dunes behind them block off the shore and there is only the wide, jade Gulf before them and the buffeting of wind and the cry of seabirds, and she and Michael have been together for months now, months, and they are in swim suits and they've been at the beach all afternoon and they've been drinking wine—quite a lot of wine perhaps—and they are standing side by side, their bare legs touching, just their legs, ever so lightly, and out before them on the water, far out, is a fishing boat, a private thirty-footer, and Michael has been watching it for a while, and he says, "My dad liked to fish the rivers and the lakes, but not the Gulf."

Kelly looks at him. He has not turned his face to her to speak; he is still watching the boat. And he did not even begin with the declaration of his father being a fisherman; he has spoken as if that has already been established, as if he has been speaking of these issues already, though he has not.

"It's a different thing," Michael says. "It made him uneasy."

He falls silent. She watches him watching the boat. And she says, "After all these months, that's the first thing I've heard you voluntarily say about your dad."

He looks at her. "I don't talk about him much. I don't know why I did now. Sorry."

"Don't apologize," Kelly says. "I'm honored."

Michael looks away.

"Really I am," she says. And as Michael watches the Gulf, clearly thinking of his father, Kelly finds herself ready to speak of another thing. She's been ready for a while, but till now she sensed it was too soon. Too soon for him. Not her. For herself, she no longer even needs to re-examine her feelings, no longer needs to play the little litany inside her of all the signs. She invokes none of them now. She is aware only of a trembling that's beginning in the place in her chest where she must focus to consciously breathe in and breathe out. *Courage* she whispers in her mind. *Courage now.*

And for the very first time, she says, "Michael, I love you."

He does not look at her. He does not answer. Not for one beat. Not for another. The trembling in Kelly ceases abruptly. But before some new feeling can assert itself in her, born of the very fears that kept her from this declaration for weeks now, Michael speaks.

"He did go out there once to fish," he says, keeping his eyes on the Gulf. "A friend of his took us out in a boat. I didn't know how to interpret what I sensed about my dad. We went far enough so that the shore had vanished. There was only deep water all around, and my dad was actually afraid. It took me years to realize this. He'd be rip-shit furious if he thought I knew."

Kelly isn't sure he's heard her. Perhaps his absorption with the memory of his father blocked out her words. The place in her where the trembling abruptly ceased expands now, warmly, he has suddenly exposed himself to her, has let her see his vulnerability, this complex thing between him and his dad—she knows complex things between a child and a father all too well—and she has to do something for Michael, something, she wants to take him in her arms, but not yet, not in this moment. In this moment it seems to her the most natural thing would be to say it once more, to reassure him that way, to let him know it and share it and give it back and then they can hold each other and it will be all right for both of them. "I love you, Michael," she says.

And he says nothing. He does not look at her and he does not say a word.

Another sort of quaking has begun in the center of her, but she still clings to the simplest possibility. "Did you hear me?" she says.

He turns to her. Turns his whole body to her, putting a hand first on one of her shoulders, guiding her to face him, then bracketing her with both his hands at her shoulders. This could be a whoa-wait-just-a-minute gesture. His hands are gentle on her but he is still holding her away. It could be an oh-my-we-have-a-major-misunderstanding-here gesture. She is trembling again. She searches his face: his eyes are gentle, she thinks, as gentle as his hands. Maybe it's okay. Maybe he will speak now. She realizes she needs words from him now. She needs actual words from this man. Three of them. A classic three words. But there are no words. He looks at her and his eyes are steady and he looks and looks and she can't stand here much longer like this. She doesn't know what she will do but she can't just stay here at arm's length in this silence. Perhaps she will simply turn and run away.

But now his hands leave her shoulders and they come around behind her and he moves into her, he pulls her to him, and she makes herself believe this will do for now. This will do. She wants this to do, since it's all he's going to give, and it will do. She puts her arms around him. She turns her head and lays it on his chest and she closes her eyes and she tells herself this is good, this is very good, his taking her in his arms. And she and Michael stand there for a long while holding each other and the only sound is the sound of the water and the wind and the birds. And Kelly blinks. A bird has flashed past her. Her face is turned to the French windows. The bird is gone—out of sight into the courtyard below—and she blinks again.

And she approaches the Blanchard Judicial Building, the courthouse where Michael often appears. This is their second summer, some months after she spoke the word *love* on a Pensacola Beach. The word has not been mentioned again. She still teaches third grade in Mobile, but she and Michael are living together this second summer. Each morning he goes out in his dark suit and white shirt and she often sleeps late. He kisses her awake only barely, only enough to say good-bye, and he goes out and she sleeps and then she fries an egg for herself in Michael's kitchen and she reads and she swims in the apartment complex pool and she watches the soaps and she waits for him. But this morning he left a note on the kitchen table. He gave her a courtroom number and a precise time, a quarter past noon, and he said he wanted her there. She has never seen him work a trial and she is happy to dress smartly and do her makeup very carefully and go out to watch her man in court.

The building is ugly modern, made up of modular blocks stacked like a child would stack them, the top floor in three massive, staggered parts hanging out, threatening to topple. She passes into their shadow and through the front doors and into an elevator. She emerges on the fourth floor. Before her is Courtroom 402 and in both directions are turnings and the clock on the wall says 12:14. She lingered too long preparing for this. But in a chair beside the courtroom door in front of her sits a burly, gone-to-paunch guard. She steps quickly to him.

"Courtroom 406?" she asks.

"Turn right at the corner," he says, pointing. "Then left."

She rushes along the corridors, taking the turns. A guard up ahead sees her coming and vanishes through a door. She arrives where he disappeared, and this is Courtroom 406 and she goes in, the guard standing stiffly beside the door, making sure the late arrival won't disturb the proceeding. She is indeed late. Things are already underway.

Michael is before the witness box, his back to Kelly and the half dozen spectators scattered about in the viewing rows. But he's turning around even as a graying man in tweeds is speaking from the box and a profusely white-haired portly judge leans attentively toward them both.

"And so the three men sort of gaped, you know, and they backed away," the tweedy man is saying.

Michael has completed his turn to face the spectators, and from his position he can certainly see Kelly now, still standing at the doorway, but he makes no sign of it.

The tweedy man continues, "Then the couple . . ."

Michael raises a hand and interrupts the witness without looking back at him. "So you would describe them as a couple?"

"Well," the man says, hesitating momentarily as if trying to verify his own perception, "they were together at this point."

Michael abruptly turns to him once more. "What happened next?"

"The three men backed away, and they seemed intimidated."

"How so?" Michael says.

"They looked shaken. The man . . ."

"The man who intervened?"

"Yes. The man clearly had made an impression."

"A strong impression?"

The witness nods firmly. "Yes," he says.

"Thank you," Michael says. "I have no further questions for this witness."

The judge says, "You may step down," and the witness does, circling the stand and passing between the prosecution and defense tables, the prosecutor giving him a quick glance as he goes by. A disapproving glance, it seems to Kelly. Michael has cleverly exposed something in his cross-examination. She is getting what she often identifies to Michael as the itchy-crawlies, the term she invokes in a whisper, even if they are alone in their own bedroom, when she wants him to touch her, to make love to her, and his mind is elsewhere. His public persona has done this to her instantly.

She steps forward and sits in the back row, as the witness sits in the front.

Michael turns to the judge. "I have one more witness, your honor."

The judge nods an oversized nod.

Michael says, "I'd like to call Kelly Dillard."

Kelly would later be reminded of an armadillo. Not a deer in headlights, an armadillo. The armadillo, when crossing a road at night and being suddenly flabbergasted by an onrush of headlights, will freeze for only an instant and then it will leap straight upwards, a reflex that contributes greatly to its role as the semi-official Florida State Roadkill. Though her astonishment at being unexpectedly called to the witness stand gives Kelly that frozen instant, almost at once she jumps up and comes forward. Inside, however, she remains in that first state of suspension.

Briskly efficient in body but dazed in mind, she passes Michael with only a little sideways glance—he is looking away—and she enters the witness stand and she finds herself with her hand on a Bible and telling a bailiff that she will tell the truth, the whole truth, and nothing but the truth. She sits.

Michael is before her now. "I'm sorry to take you by surprise, Miss Dillard," he says. "But you have a crucial piece of testimony in this case."

"I do?" she says, still failing to get her thoughts to adhere to all this.

"Yes," Michael says. "The man involved in this incident, the man perceived by witnesses as being part of the couple in question, will you marry him?"

This will take a few moments to sink in to Kelly. Just parsing the sentence in her head is coming slowly.

Meanwhile, the prosecutor rises. "I object," he says. "This man doesn't deserve her."

From beside Kelly, the judge's voice says, "Overruled. You may answer the question, Miss Dillard."

And Kelly gets it, and she is ready to leap up again. But even as her eyes bloom with tears, she stays seated and straightens her spine into the part Michael has given her to play.

He is saying, "Do I need to refresh your memory? The man, Michael Hays, saved you from exposing your tits to three drunken louts in New Orleans. Do you remember him?"

"Yes I do," Kelly says.

"He's now asking you to marry him," Michael says.

Kelly wants to banter now, wants to play Michael's game, but her impulse to throw her arms around him balances that exactly, so she sits there saying nothing for a very small moment in which the judge intones, "Will the witness please answer the question?"

"Yes or no," Michael says.

"Yes," Kelly says.

The gavel bangs and the judge cries, "Case dismissed. Everyone back to lunch." And the spectators and the tweedy man and the prosecutor all laugh and cheer.

Kelly is ready for the big embrace now, but Michael has turned away, is reaching up over the bench to shake the judge's hand. Kelly waits. Michael is saying a few words of thanks to the judge, and Kelly rises, and she waits, and then Michael is passing before her and coming up into the witness box, and he takes her into his arms. They kiss.

And Kelly is forty-eight years old and she is sitting in her Mercedes, sitting at the curb across the street from that same courthouse, which still threatens to drop the modular blocks of its top floor, and she roils hotly in her head, in her limbs, and she holds her cell phone in her hand, but the welter in her won't let her work her fingers to make this call that she has come here to make. She watches the distant figures moving before the building, seemingly unaware it's about to fall on them.

And Kelly at forty-nine sits in the flower-print chair and wrenches her mind out of her car and back into this room, this familiar room, this empty room that threatens to collapse on her at any moment.

~

Michael stands beneath a gilt federal bull's-eye mirror in the front parlor of the Oak Alley plantation house, sipping a period mint julep made with brandy and sugarcane rum. He is, at the moment, alone, and he is glad for that. He's glad he can see Laurie, who is across the room, near the mahogany piano, but for now yes, he's also glad he's not with her and with the others she inevitably draws to her. She's laughing with two young women. Michael can pick Laurie's laugh out of the crowd. He enjoys her laughter along with his sense of solitude, but the solitude does not last long. Laurie turns her face to him and cocks her head, and she speaks a few more words to the two women and then begins to glide across the parlor toward him.

As she approaches, he has a brief flash of two years earlier. A cocktail party in a senior partner's Gulf-frontage house and the place is full of lawyers and judges and spouses and clerks and paralegals, and Michael finally stands alone in this crowd too: he has just finished a trivial conversation with a junior associate, who has gone away to refresh his drink, and Kelly, who was standing beside him, looking beautiful and distracted, has moved off as well. Michael is alone in a small cleared space with only people's backs to him, but now a corridor of sightline opens up, and across the room he sees Laurie. She is wearing a cocktail dress in black satin that makes her naked shoulders and arms seem radiantly white, and she sees him seeing her, and she smiles and lifts her wine glass to him, and she nods, and he nods at her, and she is looking vaguely and recently familiar now. She apparently has taken the nods as an invitation to come to him. She moves through the crowd and he has nothing in his mind about her except noting—with actual objectivity—that she is very good looking, and he concedes to himself that if his solitary respite at this boring party is to be broken, it's okay if it's by this young woman.

She arrives. She says, "Mr. Hays."

She knows him. Yes, he's seen her somewhere. He says, "Michael."

"Michael," she says. "I'm Laurie Pruitt. I work for Arthur Weisberg."

They shake hands. Her grip is surprisingly firm. He recognizes her now from a single passing glance at the office of his own lawyer, Max Bloom. Art is Max's longtime partner.

"I'm his paralegal," Laurie says.

"New paralegal," Michael says.

"Fresh," Laurie says, and she enhances the sibilance of the word just a little, flashes its double meaning.

Michael lets her know he gets this. "His fresh paralegal," he says, reproducing her enhancement of the word.

"Fresh," she repeats, lifting her wine glass to him.

And Laurie reaches Michael in the present, in the parlor at Oak Alley, and she puts on her thickest Southern drawl. "Well, Mr. Hays," she says. "You are looking downright lonely over here. Is it your political views that have alienated your fellow plantation owners? Or the cheapness of your cigars?"

"I smoke only the finest cigars," Michael says.

"And the *largest,*" she says, and she once again massages a word to open its ambiguity.

He says, "If only Sigmund Freud had been born by now, Miss Pruitt, I would have a shocking response to that comment."

"Why, whatever do you mean, Mr. Hays?"

And a cell phone rings. Michael's, hidden beneath his swallowtail coat. The faces in the room turn toward the sound, upper lips squaring and nostrils flaring in disdain.

Michael ignores the censure and quickdraws his phone to see who's calling, even as Laurie hisses, "Michael."

It's Bloom, Weisberg, Hatfield & Moore. Finally, word. Michael says to Laurie, "You know what today is."

She softens instantly, "Of course," she says, touching his arm.

Michael turns and flips open the phone before the second ring and he moves out the parlor door. "Claire," he says to his lawyer's secretary, "I'll call Max right back. I've got to step outside the nineteenth century first."

And Michael moves through the front door and across the veranda and the terrace and into the allée. He keeps walking, even after he's alone and can call Max and can hear that it's all over. He's delaying this, and he realizes he is, and since he's alone he feels free to visibly, sharply shake his head, make an overt gesture of disgust at himself, at his own weakness. And having done this, he flips open his phone and calls Max's office.

"Claire, it's Michael. I'm ready for Max."

And moments later Max is on the line. "Michael," he says. "She didn't show."

"What?"

"Kelly didn't show up to finalize."

"I don't understand,"

"Even her lawyer was taken by surprise," Max says. "He's been trying to locate her. Nothing. No answer."

"This was when?"

"The appointed hour. Eleven. Judge Fox waited till noon. As long as he could."

"Jesus."

"I hoped to have some news by now. I'm sorry to put this on you."

Michael says nothing for a long moment. It's as if he's standing there thinking, but he isn't. He thinks about thinking something about this turn of events, but there's not much actually going on in his head.

"Michael?" Max says.

"Yes."

"You okay?"

"I just want it over."

"Of course," Max says. "What was her mood the last time you talked?"

"It's been a couple of weeks. I don't know."

"We'll keep trying," Max says.

"Thanks. Yes. I have to go." And Michael hangs up.

He tries again to think this out, but his mind is still benumbed and he is mostly aware now of the drift of voices from the house and the drape of shadows from the canopied oaks above him and the sooty sweet smell of sugarcane stubble burning somewhere. He finds himself facing the house but he turns away, walks down the allée now toward the levee, and as he does, he dials the house in Pensacola.

The phone there rings and rings, and then Kelly's voice says, "I'm sorry. No one is home. Please leave a message . . ." and Michael hangs up. He dials Kelly's cell phone.

~

Distantly an old rotary phone rings. From her bedroom Kelly hears it, waking in the middle of the night. She keeps her eyes hard shut, though she is awake, though she knows the phone is ringing. She hears her mother rustle past the bedroom door, heading for the phone. Her father is sad again somewhere. Kelly forces her eyes wide open. The sunlight on the bedspread is too bright. She closes her eyes and opens them. The phone rings. Her mind clarifies. The brick wall. The wrought iron grapes. The night table. It's her cell phone, which rings again. She chose this sound. But it's distant now, muffled, and she looks to her purse lying at the foot of the bed. Her cheeks are tight with dried tears. The phone rings. She has no intention of answering it, even without thinking who it probably is. She's out of town. She's gone away. She looks out the French windows, not seeing anything, really. Did she fall asleep for a few moments? Perhaps so. The phone rings. What an oddly wrongheaded decision, she thinks, to make her cell phone sound like the phones of her childhood. And there it is ringing again. And she waits. A bird spanks past, heading for the courtyard. And she waits and she waits and the phone has stopped. The phone is silent.

Something in her has shifted. She's not sure how much. She is sad. She is somewhere being sad. She rises from the chair and moves to the night table, passing through the sunlight into shadow. It's dim here. She turns on the lamp. She picks up the bottle of Scotch. She slices the gold foil seal with her fingernail and peels it away. She pulls the black-capped cork and it resists and resists and then moves and it pops loudly. She does not have to lift the bottle to smell the dark honey smell of the Scotch. She waits. She waits, not knowing for what. Then she squeezes the cork back in, but not fully, not tightly, and she puts the bottle down in the exact spot where it was sitting.

She picks up the pills. The plastic prescription bottle is the color of caramel. She loved caramel as a child. She pushes down on the cap and twists it and opens the bottle and she shakes two of them into the palm of her hand. Pale blue, perfectly round. One is etched with the name, curving along the edge in a two-hundred-degree arc: PERCOCET. And within the arc is a large numeral 5. The milligrams. The second pill, flipped to the other side, is blank but for a deep, gaping, knife-groove through the middle.

Kelly looks at the two pills for a long while. She is aware of no thoughts, no decision going on, but finally she takes one pill out of her palm with her forefinger and thumb and she lays it carefully in the empty space where the bottle sat, PERCOCET-side up. She lays the second directly beneath, touching the one above, making the beginning of a perfectly straight vertical line. She moves the bottle of Scotch farther to the side, closer to the bed, clearing this space. She pours more pills into her palm, and she puts one carefully below the other two, and then another and another until there are . . . how many? She counts. Seven. Lucky seven. The bottle once held ninety Percocet. More than half of them are left. She takes another pill and lays it to the right of the first, and she lays in another pill below that, and another and another until she has two tight columns. Then she starts again at the top. And she refills her palm two more times. Her hands are steady, her hands are calm and steady. She builds a third column and another and she keeps building until she has seven columns and seven rows. A small, complex, scallop-edged square made up of circles. A perfect little square in the center of the night table. Forty-nine pills. She puts the half dozen still in her palm back into the bottle. She has more than enough.

She realizes she's hunched over. Her back aches. She straightens. She breathes deeply in, lets it out. She looks down at the pills. They are perfect.

She turns and crosses the room and enters the bathroom. It's dark in here and she keeps it that way. She can see what she wants. A drinking glass beside the faucets. She puts her hand on the glass and picks it up and she is about to turn and go but she catches a glimpse of herself in the mirror. She pauses, though she keeps her eyes slightly averted, as if the person in the mirror is naked in a public place, is making a terrible spectacle of herself and you want to look but you don't, quite, you do what you can to maintain a bit of her dignity even if she won't. What can you say to her? What can you say? Kelly steps out of the bathroom.

She crosses the room, sits on the side of the bed, puts the glass on the corner of the night table. She looks at the pills. They were only recently made perfect there. Leave them alone for now. She picks up the bottle of Macallan and pulls the cork and it comes out easily, making a little echo of a pop. Kelly begins to pour and whatever is being thought-out inside her makes her lift the bottle quickly. She'll have two fingers, neat, thank you. That's enough for now. Just a little warmth for now is sufficient.

She is ready to lie down on the bed. Prop herself up and drink for a while. She returns the glass to the edge of the night table—she will not risk spilling any of her Scotch—and she begins to lift her feet. But she sets them back on the floor. She looks down. Her shoes are still on. How long has she been in this room? For a while now, and her shoes are still on. She considers this. In any room that she feels is her private space, she is always instantly barefoot. Perhaps in the six weeks of cold in Pensacola in the heart of their brief winter she will wear socks around the house. That's all. But her shoes are still on. With her little black Chanel she wore her black Louboutin platform pumps and they need to come off.

She puts the toe of one at the tip of the heel of the other and nudges the shoe loose and lets it fall off her foot. It lands on its side and exposes its arterial-red sole to her. She looks sharply away. She finds the other heel with her bare toes and pries off the shoe and drops it to the floor. Kelly lifts her legs and scoots back on the bed, plumps a pillow behind her so she can stay upright from the shoulders up, and she reaches over and lifts her Macallan. She leans back and brings the glass to her lips.

Now the first taste of the Scotch is upon her, like warm dark honey, and she lets the sip go down

quickly—this isn't a glass of wine; this isn't about taste—
and she waits for the settling in: one second, two, a few
more. And then, inside, she descends into a warm sea:
first in the very center of her, in the place where she
draws this breath and the next, she feels the undulant
warmth and then it swells outward, across her chest and
up all the way to her throat and downward, as well,
even into the place where she takes a man inside her.

~

Michael kept walking after Kelly failed to answer her
cell phone, ending the call at the first sound of her
outgoing message. He could not speak to her answering machine. At this moment he could not even begin
to think what he might say to her answering machine.
He reaches the end of the allée, but he does not turn
back to the plantation house. He crosses the highway
and he goes up the angled road that climbs the levee
and he arrives at the graveled road on the berm. Before
him is the river, nearly half a mile wide here, the far
shore a dense line of trees. Upriver a ways, on the far
shore, two push boats have laid by, side by side, each
with a dozen barges at the prow. Michael shoves his
hands in his pockets and he regrets that he no longer
smokes. This would have been the moment to light a

cigarette, to keep one hand pushed into a pocket and to smoke a cigarette with the other and hunch his shoulders a little and shut the door in his head so it's just him and the cigarette and the smoke filling him like a sweet midnight fog where nobody can see him and he can see nobody. But it's been more than a decade and there's nobody to bum a cigarette from out here and he'll be okay. He's been pretty good at shutting the door on his own. He doesn't have to think about anything he doesn't want to think about. That's why he has found this high ground and has put himself in front of the Mississippi.

But this thing did not end this morning as it was supposed to, and a vision of her rises in his head like river fog. He is standing alone in the grass between St. John's Episcopal and its parish house and he is smoking a cigarette and nodding as civilly as he can to people from both sides of the aisle telling him how lucky he is. Very civilly, actually, given how badly he wants to separate himself from all this and smoke a cigarette in this hour before he marries Kelly. He feels kindly about all these well-meaning people but he just wants to be left alone for now, Kelly herself being the only person in the world he'd be willing to put out this cigarette for and talk to. Yes: he wants to talk to her even more than smoke. And he drops the cigarette and stubs it out and he heads for the parish house. He has no clear plan in mind. He's not supposed to see the bride. He knows that she and her girls are in the parish house, but restrooms are over there too and so he has to take a piss and he will just go over with that intention and if something happens, it happens.

Michael steps into the reception hall. To his left, through a half-opened door, are the sounds of women's voices. Ahead, across the hall, is a turning and the corridor to the restrooms. He hesitates. And then he moves to the doorway, very carefully approaching from a bit to the side, staying out of sightlines. He arrives, and, incrementally, he looks in.

A fluttering of bridesmaids in powder blue with others at makeup tables beyond. This is risky. But sitting at the center make-up table, her side to him, is Kelly in white. Her chestnut hair has been poodle-permed into a mass of tight curls and long twisting spirals. He has never seen her like this and she is at once movie-star glamorous, which he likes, and suddenly unfamiliar to him, which he does not. But he can see the clean sharp lines of her profile, which is very familiar indeed, which he loves to look at when she is unaware, the vision of which rests gentle in his mind even standing on the berm of the levee before the Oak Alley Plantation.

But in the parish hall on his wedding day, as Michael reassures himself by focusing on her profile, Kelly suddenly rises from her chair and gathers her gown to move in his direction. He takes a quick backward step and another and he turns and takes another step, toward the bathroom corridor. But then he stops. He came to see her. He turns again, to face the doorway.

He waits for a long moment, and he begins to doubt that she's coming out, but then she emerges and she sees him and she straightens in surprise.

"Michael," she says, the word said with a balance of abruptness and eager lilt that make it a rebuke but with a sweet taint of pleasure at the sight of him. A rebuke nonetheless, and he knows he's supposed to explain his presence without her needing to say anything more. However, he is simply taking in the sight of her in ivory silk and old lace and puffed sleeves and he goes faintly knee-wobbly at her beauty.

"You're not supposed to see me," Kelly says.

"Sorry," Michael says, very low.

"Did you come to pee?" she says.

"Yes," he says.

Kelly smiles a knowingly purse-lipped smile. "Then it's officially okay. You can see the bride and not ruin our luck if you have to pee."

"That's a sensible tradition," Michael says.

They stand looking at each other for a long moment. Just quietly looking, with both their faces placid.

Then Kelly says, "So. I was just heading to pee, as well. Are you about to or are you done?"

"Done."

"This has been a lovely shared bodily-function moment," she says. "Just like an old married couple."

Another silence follows. Michael feels calm, feels connected to Kelly in this silence. And on the berm of the levee he remembers these next few moments that way. He does not remember—nor did he notice at the time—that something dark crept into Kelly's face in this silence. She was expecting something that, because it did not happen, troubled her in a way she could not hide. But there was no need to hide it; Michael could not see a thing. For he was content now. He was very glad he was marrying Kelly Hays. He wanted to put them back onto the path everyone was expecting.

So he says, "We should save the kiss?"

Neither does he notice the lift of her now as she breathes in deep and puts everything in her head away but the ceremony. "For the altar," she says. "Yes."

Michael angles his head slightly toward his shoulder, indicating the bathroom corridor behind him. "I put the lid down," he says.

"Then I'm glad it's you I'm marrying," Kelly says.

Michael nods and turns and moves toward the door. As he walks away, all that he's been feeling about her finally registers—faintly but visibly—in his face. But his back is to Kelly, and she does not see.

And he comes down from the levee and he walks toward the Big House and ahead is a figure in voluminous white hurrying in his direction, and as Laurie approaches, she can read nothing of the news in Michael's face, though she tries hard. But he looks as if he has come from a smoke or a piss and nothing more.

"So what's happening?" she says as she draws near.

"She didn't show up," Michael says.

"To finalize?"

"Nobody can find her," Michael says, and he and Laurie are standing before each other now.

"The bitch," Laurie says. She has never expressed this sentiment to Michael, though she has felt it several major times in the last few months. But she has always hesitated to say it and now it has leaped from her unchecked and she has an abrupt stopping inside her, an intake of breath and a stopping, to see if she has made some terrible mistake with this man she is still trying to learn how to read. He does not seem to react at all except to gently take her elbow and turn her and set them off toward the house.

And Laurie finds another feeling coming out of her unexpectedly. Her fear. "If she wants you back . . ."

Michael cuts her off. "She doesn't want me back," he says.

"And you don't want her," Laurie says, feeling oddly separated from her mind and her body, saying one thing after another without the mediation of any editor in her brain. She knows the danger of this, but she can't stop.

Michael is making no comment about what she has just said. Though it wasn't a question. She said it as a firm statement, and she takes his silence as a good thing. He does not contradict her.

But relieved a bit, she is free to feel a twist of anger, and it too tumbles out. "I felt foolish in there alone."

"I'm sorry," Michael says.

"The bitch," Laurie says, and she presses her lips tightly together, both in anger at Kelly and in fear of whatever other unedited thing might come out of her mouth.

They walk on toward the house in silence.

~

Lying propped up on the bed, Kelly has just finished the last bit of her drink. She cradles the glass against her chest and looks to the French windows. The sun is disappearing behind the rooftops. The Scotch went down sweetly and did what it knows to do and it quieted her mind for a time, but it did not alter her—she did not seek that—and now that there are no more sips, she cannot simply let herself lie here and begin to think.

She sits up. She looks at the Scotch and at her pills and at her Scotch, and she stays focused on the Scotch for a long moment, and then, once more, she turns her eyes to the pills, to all the pills, to her lattice of pills. But she cannot find a readiness in her, at least for now.

She puts the empty glass on the night table and she rises and she wishes to touch things and she moves and she does, running the tip of her forefinger along the edge of the night table, disturbing nothing, and she clutches and releases the drape beside the French windows and she is at the desk opposite the foot of the bed and she pauses and she cradles a string of the Mardi Gras beads draped on the lamp, she lifts them but she hardly looks at them and she lets them fall, and she moves on and she runs her palm lightly along the top of the mini-refrigerator, which, for a moment, she hears humming, and she brushes her fingertips across the doorknob as she passes, and in the wall before her is the closed closet door and she stops.

She moves to the closet, draws very near, but she does not open it. She turns her back to it, and the door to the room opens and she is forty. It is her fortieth birthday. She comes through this door and Michael follows her, and Kelly can see her own face passing by and it startles her, the tension across her brow, the narrowed sadness of her eyes. Michael follows, opaque as always, carrying his own brief-case—he has brought work with him—and Beau follows with the bags.

Beau has been talking without cease. "You all look very familiar to me. You've been here before. A few times, yes?"

"Yes," Kelly says.

Michael motions Beau to the closet.

But Beau stops just inside the door, apparently unaware of Michael's gesture. "And it's always this room, isn't it," he says. "Very romantic."

Kelly feels a twist of irony at the word.

"The closet," Michael says, gently though, being patient, and Beau heads where he's directed.

Kelly stops at the foot of the bed. She looks at this place where she and Michael began.

"I never forget a face," Beau says. "Names always, but never a face. I can read them, you know. Read everything in them."

And Beau chatters on about his palmist aunt on
Esplanade from whom come his powers and Kelly tries
to read the bed. The life that has evolved between her
and Michael has surely left its traces here. And she has
come back now. She wanted to come back now. They
first made love in this bed, and she felt very close to
him then, close even to his silence.

"You or me?" This is Michael's voice and Kelly
turns to him and Beau is gone and Michael has opened
the closet door and has unfolded the luggage stand
against the wall and he is waiting. Kelly doesn't answer,
and Michael clarifies, as gently as with the chattering
bellman, "Do you want to unpack first?"

"No," Kelly says. "You go ahead."

He turns to the job.

Kelly looks back to the bed, but there have been
a thousand couples in that bed since their Ash Wednesday sixteen years ago, and she turns away, moves to
the French windows, opens them, presses against the
iron railing and leans out just a little, just enough to
feel as if she's left the room. And it is her wedding day.
Kelly at forty remembers her wedding day, and Kelly
at forty-nine goes with her. She is crossing the preparation room in St. John's parish hall and she arrives at
the makeup tables and she sits at one, beside Katie, her

matron of honor, who is unsheathing her lipstick with a focused intensity that Kelly recognizes as her sister coping with nerves.

Kelly looks at her own face in the mirror. She turns instantly away, as you might look away from a friend who is in trouble but you don't know what to say to her. Though her lips are just fine, Katie is painting another layer of color onto them. Kelly waits. The waiting is all right. Kelly doesn't know if she really wants to speak this thing inside her. Katie finishes and starts again. Kelly sets up a little test: if Katie ends now with this layer, I'll speak; if she goes on, I won't say a word.

And after a few more strokes and a compressing of the lips, Katie sits back in her chair. She twists her lipstick into the tube and caps it. And now she is aware of Kelly watching her. She turns to her sister.

"What?" Katie says.

Kelly has no choice. But she backs away a bit. "I ran into Michael."

"Here?"

"Yes."

"Did he see you?"

"Yes."

Katie shrugs. "The bad luck's just superstition. Don't worry about it."

"I realize that," Kelly says. And she does, of course. This isn't the issue. She lets Katie read her, as her sister knows to do.

"What, then?" Katie says.

"Do you think he loves me?" Kelly says.

"He's marrying you," Katie says.

"Yes."

Katie looks closely into her sister's eyes. "Are you asking if *you* love *him*?"

"No," Kelly says. "Not that. I do. I love him crazy much. That's why I worry."

"Why would you doubt it?" Katie says.

Kelly could pick at the word *doubt,* but she doesn't. She says, very softly, "He's never said it."

"Never?"

"Never the word," Kelly says. "He's never used the word."

A man slides silently, simultaneously, into both their minds. Not an image—there's nothing specific to see in this regard, no memory, just a void—but they both have a sense of him now—their father—and then he passes on through, he's dressed up and waiting in the church and on this day he'll play his father role as it should be played, and he instantly passes from their minds.

Kelly says, "Your Danny uses the word."

"Yes."

"I'm glad for you," Kelly says.

"Look," Katie says. "You should talk to Michael about it."

This is the obvious advice, of course. This is good advice. They both know that. But Kelly says a thing now that, as soon as it's said, the two sisters understand to be surpassingly true in this matter.

"I can't," Kelly says. "If you have to ask, it doesn't count."

~

Far off, the cry of a train whistle. Kelly blinks in a room now no longer bright. Not yet dim but no longer bright. The train whistle cries again, distantly, from the riverfront. The sun, though still out there somewhere, has slipped behind the rooftops of the Quarter. A moment ago she was preparing to be married, she was leaning out above the courtyard on her fortieth birthday and remembering her wedding day and she came back into the room and she lay in bed beside Michael on that day. And this little afterimage plays in her mind now, with one Scotch in her and the rest of the bottle and the pills waiting and the room going dim: there was a train whistle. After she unpacks, she comes to the bed and Michael is propped up on the side nearest the night table and he has papers on his chest and he is wearing his reading glasses and she lies down beside him and he says, without looking up from the papers, "I'm sorry. I have to do this."

"It's okay," Kelly says.

And then the train whistle. And it makes Michael lift his face toward the French windows. But only for a moment. He takes off his reading glasses and turns to Kelly. "Happy fortieth," he says.

"Thanks," Kelly says.

"We've still got time before the dinner reservations," he says, as if that would be the qualm she might have with his working at this moment.

She nods—ever so faintly—more to herself, about him—but he clearly assumes that she totally understands, and he puts his reading glasses back on, and she looks away as he returns to his papers, and then the train whistle sounds once more.

Kelly leans back heavily against the closet door. Something needs to change now. Something needs to happen. She straightens. She moves. Across the floor, past the bed. She stops briefly before the open French windows. The sky still holds much of its brightness, though the sun is invisible now and the slate roofs have gone twilight dim and the dimness plunges into the courtyard before her. The French Quarter smell is changing with the sinking sun, a coolness comes on, the long-rotted food smells and the old piss wane, and ascending are the smells of the masonry and the river and a hint of some fresh food cooking, a roux, frying oysters. These are good smells, she knows, but they make her sad.

She turns away and moves to the night table and she looks once more at the pills and the bottle of Scotch. But only for a moment. She slips her shoes on, she picks up her purse, she crosses to the door and she goes out.

~

The festival evening has moved fully outside now, onto the slate terrace, where a five-piece salon orchestra is playing a medley of Louis Moreau Gottschalk, and oyster shooters float around on silver trays in the gathering twilight. Michael slides a shooter into him, happy the Oak Alley people have put in a good Russian vodka instead of trying to find a period equivalent. He sets his empty glass on a passing tray but palms a no-thank-you to the bearer who stops to offer another. Michael will drink no more tonight, except for a little wine. He needs to talk to Kelly and he wants to be clear-headed for the night with Laurie. The floodlights come on. When the last of the twilight dissipates, he'll try Kelly's cell phone again. Soon.

"Look at that," Laurie says, low.

He looks at her instead. But without even glancing his way she knows he's going to stay fixed on her instead of following her gaze—she likes that he will do this and he likes the elegance of the next gesture: she simply lowers her face, just a little, to discreetly point toward what she wants him to see.

"It's so sweet," Laurie says. He looks. The personal injury lawyer and his wife are sitting at one of the dinner tables, the only couple not milling with the drinks and the music on the terrace. They have pulled out two chairs and are facing each other and he has reached around her neck and is clasping a necklace.

"Remember?" Laurie says. "It's their anniversary."

Michael doesn't remark on the scene, but he can hear the sentimental ooze of Laurie's tone, and he waits a couple of beats before turning away so she won't think he's being critical of her feelings about this.

Laurie pitches her voice even lower, and the ooze morphs into a firmer tone of downright admiration. "I think he's got tears in his eyes."

Michael cannot avoid looking back at this.

Madison Murray is indeed wiping at Jason Murray's tears, and she is beaming. She leans forward to give him a kiss.

"That's so sweet," Laurie says, and Michael turns away again, sharply.

Laurie looks at him. She smiles and nudges him with her elbow. "My tough guy doesn't approve."

Michael shrugs.

Laurie says, "Haven't you ever shed a tear for the love of a woman?"

"I should try that call again," Michael says.

"Not for her you haven't," Laurie says. "Of course not."

Michael starts to move away but Laurie puts her hand on his arm to stop him. "I don't like being left here alone," she says.

"Do you like my staying married?"

Laurie nods once, firmly. "Okay. I get it."

Michael shifts his arm to disengage from her hand, but she holds tighter.

"Not so fast," she says. "Give me a kiss first. A good one."

He takes her into his arms. "This isn't exactly an antebellum public act," he says.

"I don't care," she says. "Kiss me right and I'll even let you flash your cell phone all you want."

And he does kiss her right, and for longer than she expected under the circumstances, which she understands to mean that she is crucially important to him, that she has nothing to fear from this wife who did not know how to love this man that Laurie adores. She lets his lips go and he turns and she watches him move away, and she just knows for sure—without it ever having needed to be mentioned—that it was a bona fide act of love for him to put on that swallowtail coat for her.

Michael passes Madison and Jason and he does not look at them directly, but in his periphery he can see them leaning into each other. Laurie was right that he doesn't approve, and he holds on for a moment to a little surge of fellow-male disgust. This is part of a deep reflex in him. And briefly maintaining a low-grade distaste for Jason Murray allows him to pass on down the allée without a flare up of any conscious image at all of a day and a night long ago in an open canopy forest along the Blackwater River near the Alabama border. However, Michael's passage now into the gathering night shadows of the trees of Oak Alley does make a deep sandbottom current of the river run in him. And in that current is a Remington .243 Youth Rifle and he holds onto it tight for a long panicky while and then he's not even aware he's carrying it and he drives forward through the wire grass and gallberry and all about him are the pine and the oak and the sycamore, and the trees huddle up and they crowd into him and he no longer has any idea what direction he's going in. He's eleven years old and he is lost and he hears a thrash and he stops and he wants to see his dad coming out of the forest to him but instead it's the back-flash of a whitetail deer and Michael doesn't even think of the rifle in his hand, he only wishes he knew where to run, like this animal, and he pushes on and on and then he emerges into a tight little clearing. He must have been calling out for his father but he's not sure—he can't remember his voice—but he does call now. "Dad!" he cries. And again, "Dad!"

And his father's voice comes to him in return, from somewhere behind him in the forest. "Michael! Stay put!"

Michael does not move. He stands very still, as if he and his father have read the deer rubs and the tracks and they are ready to hold still and wait. Michael will wait as still as his dad has taught him to wait. And Henry Hays comes out of the woods and Michael is not even aware that with his first step toward his father he has dropped his rifle and he takes that step and another and he is running and he opens his arms—he yearns to throw himself upon his father and hold close to him— and now his father looms above him blocking out the forest but something comes upon Michael's shoulders and blocks him to a stop and thrusts him back and he is thrashing from his father's hands.

"Pull yourself together," his father says. "What's got into you boy?"

"I was up ahead of you . . ."

"I mean now," his father says. "Are those tears? Are you actually crying? And you drop your rifle? I can't believe this is my own son. Pull yourself together."

And Michael seizes up, stiffens and goes dead cold, perhaps as a whitetail would feel raising its head and seeing a muzzle flash. There are indeed tears in Michael's eyes and his rifle is not in his hands and in this first deer hunting trip with his father he has failed utterly and he cannot make anything about his body work, he cannot speak or move or breathe, and his father's deep-forest-dark eyes are wide with something that Michael cannot bear to look at. But he cannot look away.

Henry Hays releases his son. "Stand straight now," he says sharply.

Michael struggles to do this.

"Listen to me," Michael's father says. "We come into the woods and we take the lives of animals, like men have done since the beginning of time. You have to honor who you are and your responsibility in the world. You can't do that with these tremblings and hugs and these disgusting tears. God put you on the earth to be a man. So be one."

And in spite of how he has strayed and panicked and cried and even abandoned his nascent manhood in this forest today, Michael suddenly grows quiet inside. He can still do this. For all but one of the several times in his coming adult life when Michael will remember pieces of this day, this will be his primary impression: his father made perfect sense; his father was surpassingly reasonable.

Though once, late at night in his law office, soon after Sam had been born, after a good day in court when he knew what questions to ask and when to push them and when to turn and walk away and dismiss the lying son of a bitch in the witness box, Michael finds his father in his mind and he has the impulse to turn his lawyerly skills on his old man, to see if his reasonableness will hold up under cross-examination: so he and Michael are standing in that clearing, and his father has just finished his little speech about manhood, and Michael says, "How did I get lost?"

"You are a child still," his father says. "No man. You wandered off like a child."

"I was walking ahead of you as you told me to do."

"You need to learn to stalk a deer."

"I was moving slowly," Michael says, "watching for rubs and scrapes and tracks."

"Like I taught you."

"If I was moving slowly ahead of you, where you'd put me, following only the spoor of our prey, how was I responsible for wandering off?"

His father falters, like a lying witness in the box. "You are a child."

Michael waves off this answer. "Where were you?" he says.

But he doesn't let his father answer. He has no more questions. In his mind he turns and walks away, walks away from this: that his father fell back deliberately to test him, that it was all his father's contriving. But what does that matter? Michael still failed the test. He had to learn the lesson, yes? His father had to do this to teach him.

And on the night that followed the day of Michael's humiliation, he and his father have pitched a tent near the river and Michael has brought some homework to do in the tent by the kerosene lamp, and he imagines he is Henry Clay teaching himself the law as a young man, and he is glad for this tent and the dim light and his father outside, glad his father brought him here in spite of what happened.

Michael rises and steps out of the tent. The dark tannin water of the river has a bright black sheen in the moonlight. His father is sitting on a log, smoking a cigarette, his back to him. From all of this—even from the reprimand—Michael fills with a thing that he is ready to give a name to, and he comes forward, he opens his arms, he will throw his arms around his father from behind and he will say he loves him. But his father, of course, hears his approach, slightly turning his head, showing just a bit of the side of his face.

Michael stops. His father's alertness to him makes him lower his arms. But Michael still wants to say this thing, wants to name the feeling, wants to say *I love you*. "Daddy," he begins, and he pauses ever so slightly to work up to the words. And he loves his daddy so much he takes pleasure even in the hesitation, in starting the sentence once more by naming him. "Daddy, I . . ."

But his father abruptly raises his hand. "Don't say a thing." His voice is firm, his voice is the voice from the clearing, and the words vanish from Michael. He feels the same stopping in him that he felt at his father's first rebuke today.

And then his father surprises him. The man pitches his voice low and mellows its tone. Almost gently he says, "Come sit here beside me."

Michael swells with the feeling he felt he needed to say, but because of that very feeling, he obeys, simply obeys, he comes around the log and sits beside his father as close as he dares, almost touching, almost but not quite touching, and he waits.

And his father says, "Words spoil it. They spoil it completely. You understand?"

Michael shakes his head yes.

A silence falls briefly between them. And then, still gentle, his father says, "Just listen to the forest."

Michael tries, though there is a racing in him now. He's trying to understand. It's mid-autumn. The forest is quiet. But the quiet has a density to it that begins to register in Michael as a sound. He closes his eyes. Deep in the woods he can hear the fluted whinnying of an owl.

"And watch the stars," his father says.

Michael opens his eyes. He lifts his face. The sky is vast above him, and it is dense with stars, and it is utterly silent.

~

Kelly has walked away from Bourbon Street, stepping from the hotel and going to her left, into the dim lakeside half of the Quarter, but she turned away from Rampart, headed first toward Esplanade and then at

some point back toward the river. Not that she is thinking any of this out or is even aware at all of what street
she's on. There are things to decide. This much she
knows. Things that don't involve thinking, not at all, and
so she has come outside into the early evening scent
of the Quarter and she is drawn forward by the quiet,
hazily lamppost-lit streets, moving past the shuttered
casement windows of the shotgun houses and Creole
cottages. But up ahead, on a corner, is the neon of a bar
and a soprano sax riffing up out of a bass and a drum
and Kelly has walked enough and she thinks to turn
in there, she'll go in and sit and she'll drink a little bit
more and see what the music will say.

And she does go in, not even looking at the few
people scattered about—missing a sizing-up from a
vaguely handsome, fortyish local bar denizen—and
only briefly glancing at the little stage at the far end
of the room, with a heavy woman in a black tunic dress
at the microphone waiting for the boys behind her to
finish their solos.

Kelly sits at a table. A young woman with a bruise-
colored garland of a tattoo circling her bicep asks what
she wants and Kelly says a Scotch with a little water
and the singer sings the final chorus. Weary blues have
made me cry, she sings. And she's going to say goodbye
to those weary blues, and though she knows she won't

forget them, she'll be bidding them goodbye, a notion that the singer sings again and again until the music ends to a smattering of applause, and Kelly wonders how you can bid your blues goodbye but not forget them. The singer announces it's time for her to take a break and *drink* her blues away and someone laughs and the bar falls briefly silent, and Kelly's cell phone rings, muffled, faint, from inside her purse.

This is Michael. He is standing beneath the oaks, shaking off an unease that he attributes to the unresolved divorce and Kelly run off somewhere, and those thoughts are part of it, certainly, but he does not recognize who it is that has been lingering in the shadow of the trees on this autumn night with the river nearby. The phone has rung and it rings again.

And Kelly has it in her hand and she turns the ringer off, once and for all. She pushes her hand into her purse, burying the phone deep inside. She closes the purse and drops it out of sight onto the chair facing her.

A male voice says, "It's a good thing that didn't happen a minute earlier."

Kelly looks up into the face of a man, fortyish, vaguely handsome in a gaunt way, he reminds her of someone that once thrilled her, from a movie, an Altman movie maybe, *Nashville,* Keith Carradine was the man that thrilled her when she was just turning sixteen.

Michael doesn't look like Carradine, she thinks. But she herself hasn't thought of Carradine for many years, until this gaunt man stands over her and he has a drink in each hand.

The man says, "Nettie packs a derringer and she's been known to use it on cell phone owners if they interrupt her song."

In spite of the man making her think of her hormonal sixteen-year-old self—and maybe because of it—she's not sure she's up for this. But she doesn't have the impulse energy at the moment even to lower her head. She looks at him, saying nothing.

He lifts the two drinks, the right hand first. "This one's mine." He lifts his left hand. "This one's yours."

Her drink? Kelly does turn her eyes now, toward the bar, looking for the waitress.

"It's okay," the man said. "It's the one you ordered. I'm just paying. If that's all right."

Kelly looks back up at the man. She can find no words. But she hears Carradine singing in her head. "I'm easy," he sings. "I'm easy."

The man takes Kelly's silence as consent. He starts to sit down opposite her, finds the chair engaged, puts the drinks down—Kelly's in front of her, and his before this chair. "Do you mind?" he says, not waiting for an answer, lifting her purse and putting it on the table, pressing it up against the wall to make room. He sits.

"I'm Luke," he says.

Kelly pulls the Scotch with a little water to her. She takes a sip. She says nothing.

"You local?" this man Luke says.

Kelly closes her eyes to the hit of Scotch. It's not very good Scotch and she has watered it down. She's still not ready to fully let go. But it feels familiar spreading into her chest, nonetheless. Warm.

"A tourist?" Luke says.

She opens her eyes and looks at this man. It's the man's long face, long thin face, the precise square of his chin that she's been struck by. "I'm just passing through," she says.

"I'm from New Orleans quite a few years now," he says, "and I talk to a lot of folks. But I don't think I ever heard that one."

Kelly tries to concentrate on the man across the table. Something doesn't fit. Keith Carradine had a little beard in that movie, and long hair, not like this man at all. She sips at her drink again.

Luke has waited a few moments for a response, but she is saying nothing. He shrugs a very small shrug and says, low, afraid she's heard him as argumentative, "The Quarter just don't seem like a place you

happen to end up in going from point A to point B."
He pauses again.

Kelly looks at him. It's from some other movie.
Short hair. No whiskers. A film by an Altman pro-
tégé, Alan Rudolph: *Choose Me*. Choose me. I'm easy.
She feels Michael next to her in a theater somewhere.
Mobile. They saw that movie together, early on. Carradine didn't look all that great to her by then. Too
lean. Hungry. Simply hungry. She was glad. She put
her head on Michael's shoulder. Choose me. She feels
tears coming to her eyes.

Luke is saying something. "You're feeling scuffed
up tonight," he says, very softly. "I'm sorry."

Kelly hears his words, appreciates the sudden shift
in him, but she can find no words of her own.

Luke says, "I'm going back over to the bar now.
If you need to just talk, you give me a sign." He rises,
picks up his drink.

"Thanks," Kelly says. Thanks for going away. He
turns. He goes. And she is sitting in her Mercedes, sitting
at the curb across the street from the Blanchard Judicial
Building and she roils hotly in her head, in her limbs,
and she holds her cell phone in her hand, but the welter
in her won't let her work her fingers to make this call
that she has come here to make. She watches the distant
figures moving before the building, and she lowers her

eyes and she finally makes her forefinger move—her finger is trembling, however, her whole hand, as well, is trembling—she can barely draw a breath—and she begins to dial.

And she drags herself back into this bar on some corner of probably Bourbon Street—she's probably made her way to Bourbon Street—and she still can hardly draw a breath. It's the bar now. It's the bar that won't let her breathe. She pulls her purse to her, feels around for her wallet. She takes out twenty. Enough for the drink. She puts it on the table and she rises and she moves past the bar without seeing anyone there and she goes out of this place and she crosses what is probably Bourbon Street because Bourbon Street won't let her breathe either and she heads down whatever cross street this is, heads in the direction of the river.

Soon, though, she is diverted uptown by a lit window in a closed antique shop on Royal and she casts her eyes over the things there without seeing them, but without seeing anything inwardly either, and she drifts on and a tune plays in her head—weary blues have made me cry—just those few bars over and over—and she wonders if she will wear a blister on her heel from walking and walking in her Louboutins and she wonders why she wore them and she wonders if she packed any Band-Aids to put on the blister that she will probably rub onto her heel but of course she didn't and she wonders why she should wonder such a thing does she think she's a tourist come to the Quarter with all the things packed that she needs instead of come here simply to move from point A to point B and she hums and thinks about her feet and about the faint dryness in her mouth and then the shops vanish and beside her is an iron fence and she stops and looks and it's Jesus standing in a floodlight at the back of the cathedral and his arms are raised above his head and his hand is broken, his hand is broken by Katrina and still unhealed, and she thinks that FEMA should take care of Jesus, that FEMA should heal his hand, and she finds herself backing away from him because Jesus does not approve of her and she is sorry for whatever she has done and whatever she might do and for whatever she is doing even now and his arms are raised as if in a blessing but his eyes are cast up Orleans Street toward Bourbon and he does not even notice her and that is just as well. She backs off. She turns and enters the darkness of Père Antoine's Alley and emerges upon Jackson Square and she could look only a little to her right to see the bench where she and Michael sat but she did not mean to come here and she angles off to her left to get away, moving quickly, and her mind has clarified enough in this escape to hear the voice of a heavy woman sitting in the darkness with a tarot deck and the faint flicker of candles before her on a small table.

"I will read your future," the woman says.

"You'll get it wrong," Kelly says, and she moves as fast as her Louboutin platform pumps will allow her to go, which isn't very fast, and when she is far enough away from the tarot reader so there can be no more discussion of her future, Kelly stops and takes off one shoe and then the other and hooks her fingers in them to carry them. And she feels the cool press of stone on her bare feet, feels it for a long moment, a good thing. Then she moves along the galleried Pontalba and abruptly she is before another place where she did not intend to go: the pavilion of the Café du Monde, lit bright in the dark, and a young man and a young woman are before her, not someone from the past but uncomfortably here before her right now and they are sitting near the street and they have pushed their chairs side by side at the tiny bistro table and he sips his coffee and she takes a bite of a beignet and she struggles to manage the powdered sugar and he watches her do this and she catches him watching and they laugh and he leans to her and puts his lips near her ear and he whispers something, her face softening as he does, and she smiles, and Kelly knows exactly what he has said, she knows exactly what he has said that pleases her, and

Kelly turns abruptly away and she moves quickly along the river-edge of Jackson Square where the carriage horses are stinking and nickering all along the curb and she cuts in front of one and crosses Decatur Street and now she is in a neutral place, a place with nothing of her and Michael: she crosses the street-performance space before the wide, low, concrete façade of Washington Artillery Park.

She climbs the stairs before her and another set of stairs up the façade and she is on top of the monument. A Civil War cannon on a pedestal aims at the Mississippi. She goes down the back stairs and finds herself crossing railroad tracks—the train whistles come from here, she thinks—and she presses on, climbing more stairs. She stops. The river is before her, going black in the gathering night and scattered with lights from Algiers across the way.

She's having trouble controlling the heave of her chest. She has rushed here, she realizes. Since she crossed the street she has been moving very fast, free to do so with her feet bare and feeling compelled to see the river. And now she pauses. She struggles to slow her breathing. She is standing on the Moonwalk, the herringbone-brick esplanade along the water, and she can't think why she was in such a rush. There's only a wide darkness before her and she turns in the direction of Canal Street and she walks on. And like her husband, the past runs strongly in her, carrying her feelings about her husband, about her marriage, about her life, but it courses in her deeply enough that it's as if it weren't there, as if she were unaffected, as if she were merely here, in this present life, choosing to take this step and then the next, moving, in this moment, for instance, toward the distant steamboat Natchez lit up bright at its mooring and toward the even more distant hotels and the bridge to the West Bank. But in fact Kelly is beside another river, the Alabama, and she is five years old and Katie is nine and she is a prissy bossy big sister such as to drive Kelly crazy and the two of them and their mother are sitting on a blanket on the grass and Katie has taken over—even from Mama—taken over the laying out of the sandwiches clenched tight in Saran Wrap and the napkins and the bags of Fritos and Mama is sitting at the edge of the blanket and she's looking away and Katie is in the center and acting like she is in charge and everything is done.

"We're not ready to eat," Kelly says. "We need Daddy."

"He's thinking," Katie says.

And it's true that he has gone off by himself, and Kelly does not look in his direction now—directly behind her, a few dozen yards away, very near the river, very near the water, almost at the edge of the water—she does not look because she is already quite aware of the fact that he is thinking, but that doesn't mean things are the way they should be when a family goes on a picnic and decides it's time for food.

"I'm not eating without Daddy," Kelly says, loudly, so he can hear. Katie has been speaking in hushed tones.

And Kelly's mother speaks now in the same hush. "Your sister's right. He'll come when he's ready." She has not even turned her face in order to take sides with Katie. She is still looking away, although not quite toward her husband.

Katie picks up the sandwich in front of her and begins to peel the plastic away. Finally Kelly's mother arranges herself on the blanket, though without looking directly at either of her daughters, and begins to pull open a bag of chips. All of this is too much for Kelly. She grabs her own sandwich and jumps up and turns away from these silly people and her mother hisses her name at her but she is already moving away, moving quickly across the grass to the massive-shouldered hunch of her father.

She arrives behind him and pulls up, her desire to be near him suddenly pressed back by the force of his self-absorption. She hesitates now. But she wants this too much. "Daddy," she says.

He does not answer, does not move. And the gravitational poles abruptly shift: what pressed her back before—his silence, his inwardness, his obliviousness—now pull her powerfully toward him. She circles him, moving into the narrow space between her father and the water, and he lifts his face to her.

She has heard already many times: you have your father's eyes. When she was toddling with language, a question formed inside her and she held it close to her for some days until one night at bedtime she stood before her father, ready to go off with her mother, and she was seeking his ritual kiss, which he would give her on the forehead, but before he even began to lean toward her in his deliberate, slow-motioned way, she asked him the question at last: "Daddy, do I have your eyes?" And he did not say a word. Instead, he pulled her hands out before her and turned them over, palms upward, and he reached with his own right hand and plucked at his eye, closing it at once, smooth-lidded, and he doubled the hand into a gentle fist, and he held the fist over her left hand and opened it, and then he closed her hand. And he did this with his other eye, just the same way, and after he closed her other hand and both his eyes had vanished before her, she dared not move: she had his eyes, she had them in the palms of her hands—she could feel their shape, their weight there—and she did not move, and she barely let herself draw a breath, and they stood there before each other for what felt to Kelly like a long time, like a very long time, like a very very long time, and after a while she began to tremble from what she held, from what she was responsible for. So she lifted her right hand and brought it forward very carefully, and she turned it, and she put her fist against the place of his left eye, and she opened her fist, and she felt his eye pop open beneath her palm. She took her hand away. Her father's left eye was restored. She brought forth her left hand, and she restored his right eye as well. And he looked at her with those eyes. For another long time, he looked at her, and his eyes did not blink, did not move. They held not the slightest trace of anything she could ever possibly read.

And now again, his large, wide-set, deep-winter-midnight eyes—so much like Kelly's eyes—as a child certainly but even more clearly so as an adult—his eyes beside the Alabama River, with the five-year-old Kelly standing before him, are empty of any emotion Kelly can perceive. And she holds out her hand with her sandwich, and she says, "Time to eat. Take mine."

And he reaches up and he takes the sandwich from Kelly, and she feels a sweet leaping inside her. But he immediately lays the sandwich on the grass beside him, and the leaping stops in her, everything stops. Though his eyes are open upon her, they have vanished and she does not have them, and so she does what she wants most to do, what she has come here, actually, to do. She falls forward onto him, her arms going around his neck and her head pressing against his, and she says, "I love you, Daddy," and she wants him to speak, wants for him to draw her even closer and to speak, to tell her this thing that she has told him. But instead she feels her wrists clasped tight, feels herself being peeled away, and her father's hands grasp her under the arms and her body moves backward and upward and her father is standing up now and she floats before him, his arms extended, holding her away from him.

He is smiling. A thinly stretched, barely upturned smile. It is, nevertheless, perceptibly a smile, and this is all that Kelly sees for now, and it balances her disappointment in failing to evoke the words she wishes to hear—words she has not yet heard from her father—not ever ever ever—and the smile even balances the fright of this sudden physical state she finds herself in. And in this balance her feelings are free to sort themselves out as she hangs in mid-air in his strong hands: she does feel his strength, she does trust him to protect her out here, she does feel safe where she is—and he lifts her higher, his smile angling up to her as she rises, and so she laughs. Kelly laughs and her father draws her down toward him—the tease, the come-here-my-baby—and then he abruptly lifts her higher, and this is a thing that once delighted her, as a toddler, when she had no words and when she knew only the strength of her father's hands and the thrill of being almost in a certain place you want to be and then abruptly not being there but knowing you are still safe and can go back again and at the very same moment your body is thrilled, is flying. She feels all that now. Her father does this once more, draws her to him and at the last moment lifts her, and she laughs again but now he does not draw her in. He keeps her far away from him, high above him, and he begins a slow turn, and Kelly looks up from her father and she sees her mother and her sister standing at the blanket, looking this way, and then she sees a distant tree line, and then she sees the river, running blue before her, running fast and wide, and her father has stopped turning, and still she hangs in the air. She looks down at her father and the smile is gone. He is looking at her steadily, carefully, as if thinking what to do with her, as if trying to decide who she is, and she hangs there above him and she says, "Okay, Daddy."

He does not move.

"Daddy, I want down," she says.

And he does not move. He does not show a thing in his face.

"Please, Daddy," she says.

Nothing.

And now her mother's voice is behind her. "Lenny." Her father's name. Invoked by her mother like this only in very bad moments.

And still he looks at Kelly as if he does not even know who she is. She squeezes her eyes shut. And she is moving. Her father is turning again with her still held high. She opens her eyes. Below her is her mother. Her father has put his back to her. Her mother lifts her face to Kelly and the eyes—which are not Kelly's eyes—she does not have her mother's eyes—these eyes below are wide and Kelly knows the feeling in them, she is beginning to feel the same thing scrabbling in the center of her chest like a sharp-clawed little animal trapped there.

Her mother lowers her face to her husband's back. She lifts a hand, but it hesitates. She dares not touch her husband at this moment. And Kelly is suddenly sharply aware of the river behind her. The river is very close behind her, the wide, fast-running river.

"Lenny," her mother says. "Put Kelly down now."

He does not. Kelly looks across the slope to where Katie is still standing at the picnic blanket, watching all this but keeping her place, waiting for things to go on in the only way she has decided they can. Kelly closes her eyes and waits too, trying not to move, trying not to cry out and flail her arms and legs. She must be reconciled to this or she will lose him utterly and that would be worst of all.

And now she is falling. Slowly. She touches the ground, and she opens her eyes and her father's face descends as well. He crouches before her, looks her in the eyes. "I'm sorry, Kitten," he says. "I was a million miles away for a minute there."

Kelly lunges forward and she throws her arms around him and she knows not to say anything and she knows not to expect him to say anything, but she tries very hard to hold him close. And with that embrace of her father, Kelly stops on the Moonwalk beside this other river. The image of the embrace has flashed into her mind as if out of nowhere, for the afternoon by the Alabama River has for all her adult life been merely a few scattered fragments. But the embrace carries with it another memory of her father that comes upon her now in its fullness. Almost twenty years ago. She and Michael stand just inside the open veranda doors of the best facility she and her mother and Katie could find, a good place, a converted, sprawling Queen Anne on wooded acreage on the edge of Montgomery, where the ones with means can come who survived, who didn't quite mean it, who everyone thinks have a chance to put this all behind them. They all wear jogging suits in muted colors. They sit in the dim parlor where she and Michael now stand. They walk the grounds. They sit on the veranda. Her father is on the veranda, sitting alone at a table, unaware of his daughter and son-in-law. His jogging suit is the color of rust.

"Go ahead," Michael says softly. I'll wait here till you want me."

"He really likes you," Kelly says.

"You two need some time alone, don't you think?"

"I suppose." The last thing she needs right now is time alone with her father. "Yes," she says.

Kelly steps through the doors and crosses the veranda. Her father's face is lowered, as if intently examining the white wrought-iron tabletop. She arrives before him. "Hello, Daddy," she says.

He looks up. And it is, of course, the same as it ever was, the very same, the eyes upon her and no way in the world to read them.

She sits in a chair opposite him. "Are you doing okay?" she says.

"Sure," he says.

For a moment she can think of no more to say. His eyes do not move from her. She needs to will this to happen, this conversation, this small talk, this enormous small talk. "Mama misses you," she says. "We all do."

"That's good," her father says.

She will not even try to figure out what exactly he means when he's sounding ironic. "How's the food?"

"Delicious," he says. "Never better."

In the brief moment she takes to get past still more irony, her father does another thing as he has ever done: a sudden softening. And because the softening is rare and always abrupt and because it always comes in the context of his impossible impenetrableness, she is, as ever, inordinately grateful for it, even as the softness, as ever, yields nothing but a minor connection. His eyes come alive and his voice goes gentle and he says, "That's a joke, Kitten."

"That's good," she says. "You're joking."

"It was hilarious from the beginning," he says.

She's at a loss again.

He reads it. "You know what I'm talking about," he says.

He means the suicide attempt. She stifles the urge simply to stand up now and say good-bye and go. But she plays the role he is so good at maneuvering her into. She cannot banter with him at moments like these. She must be the tight-ass daughter, which will allow him to be disappointed with her.

"Not hilarious, Daddy. Not for us."

He tilts his head in mock astonishment. "'The Ride of the Valkyries?' 'I love the smell of car exhaust in the morning'?"

She goes utterly blank. She might as well be the one sitting here drugged up in a jogging suit.

"I didn't actually play the Wagner?" he says.

Somehow this question sounds sincere. "Not that we knew," Kelly says.

"Sorry," he says, low, looking away. "Then it was all in my head, the joke. It's funny in there most of the time."

They both fall silent. It gives Kelly an opportunity to gather herself for what she has come here to say. "Don't do this again. Okay?"

"Okay," he says, instantly, quietly.

And this is a thing she has vowed not to press, but she's suckered yet again by his sudden softness. "I love you, Daddy," she says.

He says, "Your grandfather didn't have a sense of humor about it."

"Daddy. Did you hear me?"

"I did," he says.

And for a moment she feels a little ripple in her from the acknowledgement. It doesn't last.

"And I promise," he says. "Funny's better."

He meant he did have a sense of humor about killing himself.

"I can just laugh and leave it at that," he says.

Kelly can't do this alone any longer. She looks toward the doors into the parlor. Michael has already taken a step onto the veranda. He stands waiting for her. She loves him very much in this moment, her Michael. She lifts her chin and he instantly starts this way.

"Look," she says. "Michael's here."

Her father turns around and stands up at once, offering his hand, and the two men shake, Michael two-handed, her father putting his other hand on Michael's elbow.

"Lenny," Michael says, "what the fuck?"

"I love the smell of car exhaust in the morning," Kelly's father says.

Michael laughs loud. Leonard Dillard laughs too, just as loud. They hear themselves and glance at the muted others around them on the veranda and they choke off their laughter, which makes them want to laugh even more. They are now locked in the club room of a private male world. Kelly has vanished. She should be grateful to have this burden taken off her. She should be grateful her father is joking. But she feels tears wanting to form and this is the last thing in the world she wants from herself now and so she finds—easily finds, though it surprises her—a quick, hot swelling of anger in her at both of them. She lets that take her, and the tears vanish, and she leans back in her chair and folds her hands together in her lap as the two men sit.

Her father says, "If I was more of a hunter, I might have tried that. But I'm a terrible shot. And I couldn't figure out how to do enough damage with a trout fly."

The two men laugh again, though quietly this time. Kelly stands up and walks away, toward the parlor. If she is to be in the company of those who wish to kill themselves, she prefers them to be strangers. And it took him fifteen years to eventually get the job done. And then all of them are standing beside her father's grave. Train tracks and water nearby. Escambia Bay. Mama and Katie with their arms around each other, Mama crying quietly, Katie hardly at all. Kelly and Michael are next to each other, not quite touching. Samantha a little apart. Sam with her father's eyes. Twenty now, and how can that be? Ready to go away to try to become somebody famous. Everyone else is off getting into cars. The last few moments for the family before the hole seals up.

And Sam says, "You think the Catholics are right?"

Nobody answers.

"Is Grandpa damned now?" Sam asks.

"No," Kelly says.

"Not for this," Mama says.

And that night. The night of the day of her father's funeral, Kelly lies next to Michael in their bed in their house on the Bayou Texar, their bodies not touching, him reading papers from the office. Finishing that, from the sound of it, the rustling of the papers, the stretching of his body to put them somewhere. Her eyes are closed.

His voice. "Are you ready to sleep?"

"No," she says.

She can feel him waiting for words from her. He'd rather not, of course. About things that matter, he'd rather silence, always. She gives him silence.

"I had to finish," he says.

He thinks she's pissed that he was doing work in bed on this night.

"I know," she says.

"I'm sorry about your father," he says. "I really liked the man."

He waits for her again.

She's prepared simply to say good-night. Michael's trying here. But he is Michael. She'll thank him and she will sleep. And now something unexpected wells up in her. "Do you think he loved me?" she says.

"He was your father," Michael says.

"Do you think that's an answer?" Kelly says this quietly.

He does not reply.

"You were around us both," she says. "You're a father. Do you think my father loved me?"

"He did what a father has to do," Michael says.

Kelly hears herself. She has been in this life a long time, long enough, plenty long enough to see the irony of asking these questions of her husband, and she knows she's talking to both these men, and she knows she better shut up, she's known for a long while to shut up in these situations and she better shut up now, because she doesn't want to ask questions when she's afraid of the real answers. So she says nothing more. And she expects Michael to be true to himself and let it drop.

But he says, trying to explain, trying to be helpful, "He had his own burdens. Serious ones, obviously. In spite of all that, he did what he had to do."

And she cannot help herself. "So are you saying he loved me?"

"Yes," Michael says.

She takes this in.

And then Michael says, "Whatever that word means."

And Kelly hears one beat of her heart and another,

as if they are filling the room, and another, and Michael says, trying to be helpful, "It's just a word."

Her head is cacophonous with the beating of her heart now, and, rather like a deaf person, shaping words she cannot hear, Kelly says, "You can turn off the light."

Michael does.

And in the dark Kelly finds herself at the very edge of the water, with New Orleans vanished behind her like the setting moon. She has come down some wooden steps flanked by mooring bollards. She has stopped on the last dry step, though they continue into the dark water and she imagines she could simply descend to the bottom of the river as she would descend the staircase into the reception hall of her house, as casually as she entered the Alabama River on another afternoon, when she was sixteen, drawn to the river's edge very near the place where her father lifted her and would not put her down. There are half a dozen picnic blankets scattered on the grass behind her this time and they are filled with her yammering friends and Kelly is in a summer dress and her hair is a careful, feathered shag and she has gone off alone to the water's edge and has crouched beside it and the river is blue on this day and it races past, knowing where it is bound, to a conclusion somewhere, to a distant sea, and she rises and she steps into the water and she stretches forward

and simply lies down and she is sweeping onward in the
Alabama River but she does lift her face and she does
now open her arms and roll onto her back and look
upward into the empty bright sky and she does move
her arms now and she does move her legs—though she
knows she need not do these things, she knows she can
choose to do these things or not do these things—and
later she is on the shore and there are people around
her and she realizes her Farah Fawcett hair, which took
forever to do, is ruined. And now Kelly crouches flat-
footed before the Mississippi and she puts her arms
on her knees and rests her head on her palms and she
cannot see the water moving before her in the dark
but she knows it is rushing onward to the Gulf, which
is very very near.

~

Michael listens to Kelly's cell phone ringing, trying to
run some choices through his head of where she might
be. With her mother. With her sister. With a man. Alone
in a jazz bar on Bourbon Street with a key to Room
303 in her purse is as far from the list as the dark side
of the moon. As the phone rings, he prepares—just in
case—to keep his voice calm, to put on the tone he
would take with a crucial, frightened, reluctant witness.

It is now that Kelly turns off her phone in the bar on Bourbon Street, but Michael, of course, simply hears the phone ringing yet again and again, and then her answering-service message begins. Kelly's voice. "I'm not available . . ." And he's still not ready to say anything to her this way. Not on this day. Tomorrow maybe, if he hasn't gotten through to her. He hangs up. He holsters his phone.

He turns his face toward the plantation house. Only a perky garble of voices floats this way: the musicians seem to be on a break. He appreciates the relative quiet. He wishes he could be talking this out with Kelly now. And he thinks to call Sam. Perhaps she knows something. Sam. He turns his back on the house and walks further away from the voices and the light. Seeking a still better place to call his daughter, he slips into another undercurrent of the past. He stands at the back railing of the deck of his house, looking across his lawn at the dark water of the bayou. The deck is new, smelling powerfully of teak. The house is done at last. He and Kelly are at last in the place where they expect to grow old together. He hears the soft rustle of her behind him.

"Sam's asleep?" he says.

"She was full of chat," Kelly says, beside him now.

"The rigors of first grade," he says.

"More pleasures than rigors tonight."

"Good." He turns and, without a word, steps away from her, crosses the deck to a Grundig boombox and starts the cassette he put in late last night. Stephane Grappelli's sweet, slow, improvised jazz violin version of "Someone to Watch Over Me."

He turns back to Kelly, who has followed him part way and is now settling into a deck chair. "I'm tired," she says. "I almost finished the last of the boxes today."

He moves to the deck chair beside her, but before he can sit, Kelly says, "You should play the Ella version."

"No lyrics tonight," he says.

She hums an assent, turning the hum into a following of the tune for a few bars.

"The harpsichord is the genius touch," Michael says.

"Dance with me," Kelly says.

"I thought you were tired."

"Not too tired to dance," she says.

Michael offers his hand. She takes it and rises and they hold each other close and they move a little, slow dancing for a time with small, improvised steps. The harpsichord begins to riff with the bridge and Kelly puts her lips to Michael's ear and says, "Thank you for all this."

He stops their dancing. He pulls away just a little, enough to look her in the eyes and then to kiss her.

She returns the kiss and presses it into him, opening their mouths to it for a moment, and then they begin to dance again.

And a wee, clear voice picks up the lyric on the precisely correct beat and begins to sing, drawing out the words to fit Grappelli's ornamentations as he glides into the final repeat of the chorus. "Follow my lead, oh how I need . . ."

Michael and Kelly turn to Samantha, standing in the doorway in her Little Mermaid pajamas, as she finishes the phrase ". . . someone to watch over me."

Kelly lets go of Michael and pulls away and puts on a large, public voice. "Ladies and gentlemen, it's the famous jazz singer Samantha Hays!" She crosses to her daughter and swoops her up in her arms, saying "That was wonderful, my darling."

Michael does not move, happy to watch the two girls in his life from this place apart. He does not examine his comfort with this distance, but it is strong in him. This is his proper place. From here he can provide, protect. Nearer to them, in the sweet smell of them, in the fragile, needy physicality of them, he would only become clumsy, would only feel the demand for words and gestures he could never adequately give.

He is impressed with his daughter, proud of her. He says, "Hey, Sam. You should be sleeping."

Kelly, her back to her husband, holding her daughter close, compensating for him as always, says, "We are both so proud of our baby."

Samantha presses her face against the side of her mother's but focuses on her father. Michael nods at her, nods from this vast, sweet feeling inside him. Kelly cannot see the gesture, and Sam simply understands it to mean it's time for her to sleep.

And Michael stops beneath the trees at Oak Alley and his hand goes to his phone once more and he and Sam are at the aft gunwale of his boat, his 33-foot Bertram Sport Fisherman, pristinely new and his at last and just in time, for she is eleven, his daughter, eleven is the perfect age, and this he can do for her, this much he can do, to set her in the fighting chair and crouch beside her and show her how to use the light tackle.

"Will they be heavy?" she says, and he can hear the faint quaver still in her voice.

"You're after bait fish," he says. "You can do it."

"Then you'll catch the bigger ones?"

He palms her hand on the reel. She's going to be okay. "That's right," he says. "With the ones you catch. We're a team."

"I'm catching the babies?" The quaver has come back.

"No," Michael says firmly. "They'll be adults, but smaller species."

Samantha nods her head once, sharply, and he squeezes her hand in appreciation at her determination, though he does not understand that it is simply to please him.

She carefully readjusts her hands on the tackle.

"You okay now?" Michael says.

"Sure," Sam says.

He rises. And Samantha casts her line as he's taught her.

He will step away now. She needs to do this on her own. But as he turns, he hears her begin to hum. She quickly finds the tune and then sings, very softly, "Anticipation, anticipation is makin' me late, is keepin' me waitin.'"

He crouches beside his daughter again. This, too, he can do for her. "Don't spoil it," he says, firmly. "Be quiet and look around you. You're alone in the middle of a great sea."

Samantha turns her face to him. "You're here. And mom."

Michael says, "Inside your head. You're alone in there. Take it all in just for yourself. No words now."

Samantha shrugs and looks out at the Gulf.

He knows she can't truly see what's before her. She doesn't get it. He does not think of himself sitting next to his father beside the Blackwater River, looking into the vastness of the sky, but that night animates this present disappointment in his daughter.

He rises, he turns away from her, he steps to the center of the deck of his new boat, and he takes it all in: the vast, calm Gulf; the vault of the bright sky; Kelly lying on a plank of sunlight beside the cabin door, reading a book, very near but unaware of him; and his daughter, her back to him, quiet at last, her narrow shoulders hunched toward the Gulf in concentration.

He steps to the port gunwale and leans outward, and all there is now in the world is the water and the sky and him, as if he is alone in the world. This is a good thing. This is why he has bought this boat. He does understand the dark undertow of this kind of solitude. But he is freed from that simply by knowing they are nearby, his wife and his daughter. Nearby but unseen. He will come out here alone, and they will, in their distant existence, make it all be good. And he will at times come out with men, and the unsentimental familiarity of them, their detached maleness, will serve the same function, will let him swim free of the dark depths beneath him, will let him float here in solitude, as he is doing now, and any longing for someone else to be next to him can vanish.

And Kelly appears beside him at the gunwale, smelling of coconut, her oiled arm touching his. He keeps his face out to the Gulf.

"Which way's Florida?" she says.

"Starboard," he says.

She falls silent a few moments and then she says, "Are you thinking of him?"

Michael made the terrible mistake a few years ago, before he and Kelly were married, of speaking of his father to her, of revealing that his father had an odd fear of the open water. She has referred to this a couple of times since, and Michael has always simply ignored it.

He should do that now, or he should confront his mistake openly, but he does a silly other thing, trying to act as if he never made the mistake to begin with. "Who?" he says.

"Your dad."

"No," Michael says.

He waits for it to pass. But he wants it to pass once and for all. So he says, making his voice go soft, trying not to cause trouble, "You go too far. I should never say a thing."

It came out badly. He feels the flinch in her, but she does not reply. She simply moves away.

He's glad there won't be an argument. But he's not seeing what's before him now. His wife is stewing, and it's his fault. His father has slipped onto the boat and is trying to still the trembling in his hand on the reel. And Samantha has begun to sing to herself again.

Perhaps she is singing tonight, Michael thinks, as he stands beneath the oaks of Oak Alley. Somewhere. He shallows his mind now. He needs to know one thing and he cannot deal with the rest. Sam has understood not to press the subject, and he is grateful to her for that. And it's why he can turn to her now. He dials his daughter's cell phone. She answers after the first ring.

"Daddy? Daddy, I'm about to go on."

"Sorry," Michael says. "It can wait."

"No," she says. "It's okay. I've got a minute."

And Michael finds himself without words. He would never understand the irony of this, but his abrupt word-blankness unsettles him. When he has a purpose and the will for speaking, he trusts himself always to know what to say. It's his job.

"It's been a while," Sam says.

"Where are you singing?" It's the best he can do for the moment. He has lost his will to speak of his wife to his daughter.

"Chicago," Sam says. "A little club in Chicago."

"That's good," Michael says. "Chicago's good."

Michael can find no more small talk, and Samantha is still trying to grasp her father suddenly calling.

They stay silent for what feels to both of them like a long time. Samantha realizes she has to take charge.

"How are you?" she says.

"I'm okay," Michael says.

"Good."

And now he finds his focused, courtroom voice. "Have you heard from your mother lately?"

"Yesterday," Sam says.

"Was she okay?"

"This is all hard on her."

Michael feels a tight twist of something at this, but he does not let it deflect him from his line of questioning. "Did she say anything about a change of plans?"

"Plans?"

"She didn't show up today to finalize the divorce."

"She didn't say anything about that."

"Do you know where she is?"

"Home, I assume. I don't know."

The burden of talk slides back to Michael, but he goes silent. He has learned what he can—nothing—about what he is focused on at the moment.

"Look," Sam says, "she just called basically to say she loved me. She's sad. I don't know what else to tell you."

Michael remains silent. He would like to, but he does not know how to change the conversation now.

"Are you there?" Sam says.

"Yes."

"I'm sorry about all this," she says. "For both of you."

"Thanks."

"It's hard not hearing from you," Sam says.

"I'm sorry," Michael says.

"I have to go now. I have to sing." And sitting in the manager's office of a dinner club on the North Side of Chicago, waiting to sing, Samantha feels her stubbornness stir in her, and though she has not said it in a few years, having struggled to accept this thing in her father that she tries without success not to accept in the men she falls for, she says, "I love you, Daddy."

"Sing your heart out, Sam," he says.

"I will," she says. Easier to accept is her father's awkwardness at the end of phone conversations, so without a formal exchange of "good-byes", she hangs up, and at the exact same moment, so does he.

Michael slowly puts his phone away, trying to be the attorney about this, the engaged but detached attorney with a skitterish client. Kelly will turn up. It's in her best interest to turn up. And there is a rustling near him and a hand slipping into his arm. "Don't worry. I wasn't listening," Laurie says. "I was lurking from afar."

Michael is surprised at the quick swelling of grati-
tude he feels at Laurie appearing beside him: he likes
her hand on his arm, firm there, he likes the headshop-
dusky smell of her, likes the aggressive smartness of her,
her knowing the first thing that would occur to him,
that would threaten to piss him off though he wouldn't
show it, likes that she knows and she goes straight to it
and refutes it, he likes her turning him away from the
house now, heading them down the allée into the dark.

They walk slowly for a time without saying anything, and Michael is grateful to Laurie for that too,
especially since he knows she is prone to talk and will
start to talk soon, but she also sometimes knows to keep
quiet, and Michael puts his hand on hers in the crook
of his arm. He realizes the gesture will probably loosen
her tongue, but he finds himself ready for that, even
finds, a little to his surprise, given the circumstances,
that he will be glad to hear her voice.

She says, "No word, I take it."

"No word," he says.

"I'll keep my mouth shut."

"Good."

Laurie knows her man's predilections and believes
that knowing them and teasing about them somehow
mollifies them: she nudges him with her elbow and
says, "Only about that."

And though he meant simply that it was good she wasn't going to talk about Kelly and though it's true that he would actually like to hear her voice at the moment, he plays his role. "Too bad," he says.

She elbows him again, knowing rightly this time that he's simply posing.

They have emerged from beneath the canopy of oaks and they approach the iron gate at the highway. The house floats brightly behind them and the salon orchestra has begun again and it is all distant, like watching a cruise ship from the shore, heading out in the dark into the Gulf.

Michael and Laurie stop at the gate, turn to face each other.

She says, "I'd love to lunge into your arms right now and, you know, cling to you. But this fricking dress won't allow it."

"Now that really *is* too bad," he says.

Laurie cocks her head toward the levee and wrinkles her brow in faux philosophical thought. "But if I wasn't wearing this dress, we wouldn't be here tonight in the first place for me to wish I could throw myself into your arms."

"We'd be somewhere."

"O. M. G.," she says, full-stopping with each initial. "My man's gone sentimental on me."

"That's computerese, right?"

"'Sentimental'? Nah. Outside of Photobucket baby-animal shots, it's pretty much all petty snark out there."

Michael was willing to hear her voice, but she has a sweet tooth for bantering and he's presently not up to that. He looks away.

She says, "Oh my god. It means 'Oh my god.'"

He looks back to her.

"I'm sorry," she says. "I've got the ditz gene. You know that by now, yes?"

He doesn't answer.

"This is the wrong time," she says. "I'm sorry."

"It's okay."

"No fricking dress, and we're holding each other and I'm not saying a thing."

"You don't have the ditz gene," he says. "You've got the mimic gene. The tasty butterfly making herself look like the poisonous one. It's safer."

She reaches out and puts her fingertips on his cheek. "See why I'm crazy about you?" she says.

They stand there like that for a long moment, with Laurie simply touching Michael's face, not saying any more. He is grateful to her for this silence. Even more so because he knows it's not her natural state.

Finally she lowers her hand and, without taking her eyes off him, inclines her head slightly off to the right, toward the levee. "I think I could figure out how to climb up there with the dress. I bet there's something nice to see in the dark."

Michael opens the gate. He and Laurie cross the highway and go up the inclined road to the berm of the levee, and her hoop-skirted dress does not prevent him from putting his arm around her waist.

~

And fifty miles downriver, at the foot of another levee, Kelly rises from where she has been poised on her haunches between water and land, made simply weary, at last, by watching a river whose current she cannot see. She wants her own little room. Her own locked space. Room 303. Her ironic space. And the irony is hers. She's in on it. She is climbing the steps and crossing the tracks and climbing again and the cannon is hers too, everything she sees tonight is all hers. And she descends the front of the monument and turns away from the Café du Monde and she crosses Decatur, moving in and out of the spill of lamplight, and as she heads up the dim St. Peter Street side of Jackson Square, she finds herself on a warm spring night at a cocktail party in the house of one of Michael's senior partners, and the place is full of lawyers and judges and spouses and clerks and paralegals. Her drink is almost empty. She knows that without having to check. And she also knows she's looking beautiful. She is certainly not unaware of her flaws, her inbred flaws and the flaws of being forty-seven, but for some reason the fractional part of her that knows she can still look beautiful and even more or less young when she wants to, that part of her is in control at the moment, and maybe it's the wine but there she is, the I'm-okay Kelly, standing in this crowd and not caring overly that Michael is ignoring her.

He's speaking to an associate about John Edwards. "Look," Michael is saying, "I'm not endorsing him, but a hundred and fifty dollar haircut turns into a four hundred dollar haircut when the campaign-quality L. A. hair guy has to come to you."

Kelly drains the last bit of her wine while Michael says, "Surely, that's justified while running for president."

Kelly lowers her glass and looks through the crowd, across the room, to the bar.

Michael's associate says, "I've done a hundred and a half for the sake of a jury."

"Of course," Michael says. "It's like the lifts in your shoes."

There is a beat of silence. Kelly looks toward her husband's conversation. His back is partly turned to her.

The associate, who is not quite Kelly's height, is breaking into a smile and then a laugh, which Michael joins. The associate says, "One jury in three will acquit on just those things."

Kelly moves away, heading for the bar, excusing herself through the bodies without even checking to see if they belong to someone she knows. She needs more wine. But when she arrives before the bartender, a young man with a tattoo of a Chinese character on the side of his throat, she alters her plan. "Scotch and water," she says.

As he mixes, she turns fully around and leans against the bar. The slow eddying of the crowd opens a sightline back to her husband. The associate has moved away. Michael is alone. He is nodding to someone across the room. And now he lifts a bit at the chest, straightens up in that male way at the sudden attention of a woman, and he watches. The someone must be approaching. Kelly doesn't really care who it is, but there's nothing else to look at, and a thin, pretty blonde woman wearing a black satin bare-shouldered cocktail dress arrives in front of Michael. She seems very young. She does an awestruck little shoulder ripple and face bob. This is Michael: his upstraightness has now morphed into a tight-assed formality. He shakes her hand.

Kelly looks away.

"Scotch and water," the bartender says behind her.

She turns around, and as she puts her hand on her drink, someone arrives next to her, and a male voice says, "Scotch and water."

She looks. For a moment he is in profile. His darkish hair is cropped very close, as close as the carefully manicured scruff of his beard, and there is a thin angularity to him that she thinks is very nice. He turns his face to her and he smiles. He is, she reckons, the age that she is looking tonight. She nods and lifts her own drink to him.

"Scotch and water?" he says.

"Scotch and water," she says.

His brow furrows. "Did you oversee the proportions?"

"Bartender's choice," Kelly says.

He lowers his voice with a sideways glance. "Do I need to intervene? Did he get it right?"

Kelly glances very quickly at the bartender, who is uncapping the Scotch but looking discreetly away with the merest trace of a smile, a good bartender giving permission for two strangers to make him the subject of playful talk. She returns to the stylishly scruffy face before her and lifts her forefinger and takes a sip of her drink. She ponders a moment. "For me, it's just fine," she says. "For you . . ." She finishes the sentence with a who-knows shrug.

"No," the man says. "Really no. I sense we're the same in this."

Kelly smiles and slows herself down. Is this just bored cocktail party banter or is it flirting? For her it's banter. Perhaps for a man, the two are the same. Perhaps for this nice-faced man, it's flirting. It makes no difference. She would glance now in the direction of Michael and the blonde except the man is blocking that view, and Michael is not a flirter anyway, and she says, "I sense that too. Which means if the Scotch were good enough, you wouldn't use any water at all."

"You see? My intuition is unerring."

"Then you're a dangerous man."

The bartender sets a Scotch and water before the intuitive man. He picks it up.

"Isn't this odd," he says.

"What?"

"I can sense your Scotch and water preferences, but I'm not sure if you're one of us."

"Being?"

"An attorney."

"I'm married to one of you," Kelly says.

"Ah," the man says. "That."

"And you?"

He shrugs. "I'm one of us."

"Here with one of us?"

"Somewhere in the room."

Good. That's settled. Kelly offers her hand. "I'm Kelly Hays."

He takes her hand and shakes it with an earnest not-quite-firmness that she suspects he developed for greeting new female clients. "I'm Drew Singleton," he says.

"Mr. Singleton."

"Drew," he says, keeping the handshake going.

"Kelly," she says.

"Would that happen to be Michael Hays?"

"Yes."

"Impressive."

"He must be your boss."

"Why do you say that?"

"You broke off the extended handshake as soon as you realized he was my husband."

Drew laughs, but even as the laugh animates him, his eyes focus more intensely on her face.

"You're good," he says. "Wrong, in this case, but good."

"Like one of you."

She pauses just enough to let him try to figure this out without actually having time to do it.

"Right or wrong isn't the point," she says. "It's being good that counts."

He laughs again. He lifts his Scotch and water to her and they touch glasses.

"A whole other firm," Drew says.

And now he waits for her to puzzle for a moment.

"Not only is he not my boss," Drew says. "I don't even work in his firm."

And Kelly stops in a stretch of dark somewhere alongside Jackson Square. She tries to shake all this off. But she is at another party at another house in the summer of that same year, a large Gulf-frontage house with a major deck and pool, and many of the others are in swimsuits but she is wearing a summer dress, because however beautiful and more or less young she can sometimes feel she looks, her confidence does not extend to any swimsuit with any style at all. She is already drinking Scotch and water, though slowly, having skipped the wine but not intending to get tipsy, and she is standing on the deck just to the side of the wide sliding doors into the house. She is watching a blonde. Not the blonde who approached Michael at the earlier party, though that blonde will soon emerge from the doors beside Kelly. This blonde is across the pool and is not as young by a decade as she looks, which is about twenty-five, and Kelly is trying to figure out the signs that tell her this is so. The woman is standing with a drink and she is gesturing grandly with her free hand and the three men around her are listening intently.

And a male voice says, "We're both in a rut."

Kelly turns to find Drew Singleton beside her. He lifts his own Scotch and water. "But this is a pretty good one," he says.

They touch glasses, and they both drink.

"You remember me?" Drew says.

"Of course."

The blonde across the way laughs. It is a sharp, projected laugh, as if by a skilled stage actress in a large theater. She slaps backhanded at the arm of one of the men.

"Didn't I see you come in with her?" Kelly says.

"Quite brazenly," Drew says.

She looks at him. "She's one of us? Me, us?"

"A lawyer's wife? Yes."

"Your wife?"

Drew laughs. "Of course. I didn't really mean . . ."

"I know," Kelly says, rather firmly, feeling suddenly twitchy. "She's very beautiful."

"She is."

"You looked very good together in your brazenness." She realizes this has come out sounding oddly sad.

"Did we?" Drew says. "I love her."

And his declaration comes out flat, explanatory in some suddenly serious way.

Kelly feels a dark blooming in her, a dark dark thing. She looks at Drew Singleton, who is looking across the pool at his wife.

"I like how easily you say that," Kelly says, meaning *love,* meaning the word *love.*

At this moment, beyond Drew Singleton, a woman emerges from the house, a pretty young blonde woman in a stylishly minimal swimsuit who is, however, merely a bit of background motion for Kelly, though she would recognize the blonde from the previous party if she weren't studying Drew's face with a sudden intensity, as if she'd suddenly heard a rumor about him, a secret about him revealed—he is a man who can speak openly and explicitly, even to a near-stranger, about his love for his wife—and Kelly is compelled to look at him closely, to invest this new, insider knowledge of the man into her physical perception of him, the way you stare at the face of a celebrity for an extra few seconds when you see a tabloid revelation: behind these eyes is the capacity for *that.*

And Kelly stops again somewhere beyond Jackson Square, somewhere in the dimness between streetlamps, somewhere before some shuttered Creole cottage with a dog barking in the distance and Kelly is sitting in her Mercedes, sitting at the curb across the street from the Blanchard Judicial Building, the place where her husband becomes the man he most naturally is, the impressive man, and she is dialing her cell phone with trembling hands and she says into the phone, "It's me. I'm outside. Outside the courthouse. Please come out here. Please come out here and see me." But no more than this now. Kelly lets no more than her own desperate voice into her head before she moves on, quickly now, back toward the Olivier House and her room.

~

Michael goes up the hard-packed dirt and pea-gravel road toward the top of the levee and Laurie pushes his offered hand away as she mutters on about how this was a mistake but don't let's go back I don't want to go back I want to do this and thanks but I need two hands to deal with this dress, and what plays in Michael's head is the little scene that ends with Laurie going out the wide sliding doors and past Kelly and Drew and on toward the pool, and it is a scene as inconsequential and as incrementally crucial as the scene that concurrently plays just out of Michael's sight between his wife and a lawyer whose own wife laughs with three men at the far side of the pool. As Michael looks out those glass doors and idly wonders which lies a current client is telling him are conscious lies and which are lies the client is also telling himself, Laurie appears at his side.

"So, if I can ask your advice," she says, and she waits for him to turn to her, which he does now. He recognizes her at once, though he has not seen her since the brief first conversation at the earlier party. She is wearing a lime green chiffon mini-robe and her hair is rolled up and she has sunglasses wedged at the top of her forehead.

As soon as she has his attention, Laurie says, "If I was needing counsel, should I go with a lawyer who strips down to his Speedo and swims at a swim party or with a lawyer who stays dressed and just watches?"

"Hello," Michael says.

"Hello," Laurie says. "It's me again."

"It depends what you need him for," he says.

"I'm not stalking you," she says. "We just keep showing up together."

"I believe you."

"Good," Laurie says. "So. Yes. You were saying it depends."

"If you've got trouble with a man, go with the Speedo. If you're in trouble with the law, you'd want him to be the clothed type."

"Which are you?"

"There's no Speedo under these chinos," Michael says.

"Well," Laurie says, "if you're a watcher, I'll be swimming soon. Just to let you know." And she moves off at once through a clear space between chatting gaggles of other clothed types, and as she moves— even before she reaches the doors—she strips off the mini-robe. Michael's breath snags at the sudden flesh of her. He is happy to be living in the era of backside cleavage and bared cheeks, but happy only in the way clothed-type lawyers with the lies of clients in the forefront of their minds are capable of being happy over a matter like that, particularly when prompted to it in public places by women young enough to be their daughters.

And now he finds himself standing in an antique tuxedo on the berm of an upriver levee with that very woman and she is muttering on about her nineteenth century gown and how did they live in these things you'd think life was hard enough in the nineteenth century without doing this to yourself, and she and Michael will sleep together tonight and he is thinking about the moments when she was at her worst. Her body was lovely but she was at her worst. Her reckless flirty worst, soliciting his eyes, implicitly daring him to act. Kelly has vanished before finishing off their marriage, has gone out somewhere, no doubt drinking, and maybe not alone, and Michael is selectively making some kind of case in his head against this beautiful young woman who seems to think he's worth something. He doesn't like what his mind is doing. He reboots.

And Laurie says, "Here we are in this awesome place, and listen to me. Are you sure you don't think I've got a bad case of the chronic ditzes?"

He looks at her. Her face is bright from a gibbous moon rising over his shoulder. He's a defense lawyer, not a prosecutor. And she's a perfect client. Surprisingly smart and self-aware and honestly self-critical. "I'm sure," he says.

"I want to make you happy," she says. "I really do."

"I get that."

She lowers her face and is moved to gently plant her forehead in the center of his chest. She tries and more or less succeeds but is leaning awkwardly far forward over her hoop skirt. "This doesn't work," she says, and she straightens.

"I've been thinking about when we first met," Michael says. "No, the second time, I guess it was. At the pool party."

Laurie shudders inside and she lets it out, exaggerates it so he can see. "What you must have thought," she says.

Michael smiles at her self-criticism. This sort of thing about Laurie Pruitt is what he should focus on. This is why he's here.

"I thought you had a great ass," he says.

She slaps him lightly on the shoulder.

"Wasn't that your point?" he says.

"Of course it was. Why do I behave like that?"

"I have no idea."

"Oh right," Laurie says. "Lawyer, not therapist. I'm on the wrong floor."

"Did you see something I didn't?"

"For me to behave like that?"

"Yes."

"Something about you?"

"No."

"I knew who your wife was. I don't know what I saw."

He cuts off these thoughts. He wants simply to stand on this levee in the moonlight with this woman now.

Laurie angles her head to the side, studying him. "You're coaching me into an alibi."

He laughs.

"For my bad behavior," she says.

"You're good at this," he says.

"Do I need a lawyer?"

"You've got one."

She likes this answer. "What do *you* need?" she says. "Right now."

Michael would be willing to answer this, but the question renders him instantly dumb. He knows she is sincere. He knows this young woman truly wants to give him whatever it is.

She waits.

The long-practiced rhetorical part of him takes over. "Not to have to answer that question," he says.

The moon is bright enough for him to see her roll her eyes.

He does think of one thing. "To have the divorce over with," he says.

"Of course," Laurie says. "But how about something I can give . . . Okay. I can give you this: you don't have to answer that question."

"Thanks."

"But if I didn't have this fricking dress on," she says, "I'd give you a blow job. Right here, right now."

Michael realizes that outwardly he is showing nothing in response to this. Inside, he churns. But whatever gift Laurie has for figuring him out, she doesn't pick up on this.

"Sorry," she says. "Is it that codger lawyer in you?"

"No," he says. "On the contrary. One of the things I'm finding about you is that you know what I need even when *I* don't know it."

She lifts her hand and touches his cheek. "Maybe," she says. "But there's something. Not the codger. It's the old-school romantic in you. I shouldn't be talking like that till we've made love. I know how you want the first time to be right. I admire you for that, Michael."

~

Kelly stops before the door of the Olivier House. Nothing is decided. Not quite. Not yet. If there's any thought in her that perhaps something has been decided, any thought she can access, then her answer to herself is no, nothing has been decided. Except that she has to go to her room. But she stops before the door of the Olivier House and she looks around the street and she smells the night smells of New Orleans and there is a warm trace of boiling shrimp in the air and that's a very good thing to her, but even the faint, unnamable fetidness of the Quarter at night is good to her, even that makes the distant lamplight blur in her eyes, and she will start to weep now, weep fully and forever to the end, if she stands here any longer, so she goes up the steps and through the door and down the entrance hall and there is a smell of wood fire and she passes the door to the parlor and the flames are lashing in the fireplace and she approaches the freestanding reception desk and a woman sits there, a woman with a long drape of hair the color of dense November cloud cover and she has a thin, unmadeup face, pretty in a long-ago-flower-child way, and it is a familiar face, and the woman says, "Good evening, Mrs. Hays."

"Good evening." And though the context is obvious enough, Kelly tries to get her mind to work to summon up a clear memory of the familiar woman before her. She can't. "I'm sorry. Have you been here many years?"

"I've worked the night desk here for . . . oh my, quite a few years now. I think for just about as long as you and your husband have been coming here. I'm Ramona."

"Hello, Ramona," Kelly says. "I'm here alone this time."

"I didn't realize."

"We're separated," Kelly says.

"I'm sorry."

Kelly presses her hand against the edge of the desk to steady herself. "I say 'separated.' Not that we'll reconcile."

"I understand."

"Yes. Well. I'm going up to my room now, and I don't want to be disturbed."

"Of course."

"It was not a good ending, you understand."

Ramona puts her hand on the desk, not reaching for Kelly's but showing Kelly that hers is there if she wants to take it. "I've been through it myself, cher. I work nights for a reason."

"I'm not here," Kelly says.

"I understand," Ramona says.

Now Ramona lifts her hand and extends it and brings it very near Kelly's and Kelly takes this woman's hand and squeezes it, briefly, only briefly: she was wrong about wanting to touch someone's hand. She doesn't want to touch anyone.

She nods good night to Ramona and circles the desk and moves to the courtyard doors and she puts her hand on the latch and a phone rings behind her and Kelly pushes quickly through into the dark of the courtyard and the door closes behind her but it's too late, she is sitting in her Mercedes outside the courthouse and she has dialed her cell phone and it has rung

and she has imagined it ringing in his hand just before
he answered it and she has said what she has said, invited
what she has invited, and she has gotten out of her car,
but she leans back against the closed door, stays where
she is, and she watches across the way, far across the
way at the comings and goings at the courthouse doors,
bodies vanishing into the building, bodies emerging,
and then she thinks it's him, coming out that door, and
he pauses, and that distant face turns and looks in her
direction and he moves toward her and she straightens
and steps away from the car, but only one step, and
he is clear now, she can see the tight, scruff-darkened
contour of his face and she waits, and Drew Singleton
crosses the street and he is before her, he is very close
to her, and she thinks she can smell him, the Ivory soap
and the shirt starch of him.

And he says, "I was afraid I'd mistaken . . ."

"You hadn't," Kelly says.

"It's all terribly confusing."

"I know."

He squares his shoulders before her. "Kelly, I'm
very happy to suddenly find myself standing in the
middle of this street with you and not be mistaken.
But I have to say this first."

He pauses and his shoulders sag a little now with
a difficult thing.

"Go ahead," Kelly says.

"I still love her," Drew says. "I love my wife. I'm not sure I can leave her. I don't think I can."

Drew pauses again and Kelly holds very still and she waits for what's next, and contrary to the classic expectation in this circumstance, she's okay with what he's just said, more than okay, because it makes what she deeply hopes for in the next few moments possible, because his needing to say this thing to her in the middle of the street before they go on is the very reason he is the kind of man—though in her mind he is not a type, he is intensely particular, he is the *only* man—who brings these possibilities into her life, who reminds her how deeply these needs run, deeply enough that the risks are worth it, worth it for what she expects now from Drew Singleton.

And he goes on. "But. But. You need to know . . . Can I say this?"

"Yes." Barely a whisper this. Kelly can barely make a sound.

"I love you too," Drew says.

And everything stops inside her. If she could make this be enough, if only she could make this one time, this once, this spontaneous once, this once in the middle of the street, this once in spite of a husband and a wife, if only she could make this once be enough, she would do that, if she could kiss this man now and say good-bye and return to her life and never need anything from Michael again that he can't readily give, she would do that. She wants to do that. But she knows how impossible that is. She needs this now in the middle of the street and she needs it again and again—and soon—and she needs it while they are naked together and holding each other as close as bodies can on this earth, she needs to hear it, she needs to hear a man say he loves her, she needs that, she needs.

"Is that crazy?" he says.

"It's not," Kelly says. "But once said, it bears repeating."

"I love you too," Drew says.

"Simpler, please."

"I love you," Drew says.

And she is happy. And she is unutterably sad. And she says, "Where shall we go?"

And she is weeping now: she has moved into the deep night shadow of the loggia leading to the inner courtyard beneath her window and she has stopped and she has leaned against the stone wall and she is weeping, and she presses hard at her eyes with the palms of her hands, trying to press the tears away. She does not need to do this now, she just needs to go to her room and lie down, and if there is more to think about, she can do it there and she can decide, she can decide what to do, she can decide what she will do about what she has done, and she straightens and she moves through the loggia and into the courtyard and she is focused so intently on the steps going up to her room that she does not see the pool and she does not see the young couple who were laughing with each other and leaning into each other when she arrived this afternoon, does not see them as they are stepping from their poolside room and the young woman is wearing her black panties and black bra as an impromptu bikini and the young man is wearing his workout-gray boxers as an impromptu bathing suit because it is a warm November night and they have been wishing they'd brought swimsuits for the pool and they see this woman emerge from the loggia and they stop but they know in the dim spill of blue light from the pool that they look perfectly natural, they look like they are wearing swimsuits and they look like they are in love and they see this woman across the pool who does not glance their way and the little trepidation they had about swimming in their underwear vanishes and the young man in the couple thinks the woman is pretty and he has a faint, unacknowledged wish that she had looked his way and had seen what a pretty girl he's with and what a hunk of a guy he is in his boxer shorts and had stopped and smiled and come to them and asked if she could join them, and the young woman in the couple sees that the woman is hurrying in a focused way and she thinks the woman is going up the steps to meet her lover and is a little bit late but it will be all right because her man is waiting patiently and is full of love like this young man is for the young woman.

And Kelly climbs quickly, needing to be in her room, and she comes up to the third floor and she goes to her door and her hand is steady now, her hand puts the key in the lock at the first try and she is opening the door and she steps inside her room and she closes the door behind her and she leans back against it and her heart is pounding hard, her heart is pounding so hard it is all she can think of for a moment, how hard her heart is pounding, how strong that heart is, how stupidly strong her heart is.

Laughter floats into the room. Like the stink of the streets in New Orleans on a warm night. She remembers the young couple from the afternoon. The stupid young couple, their hearts beating strongly out there, feeling their hearts beating inside them and being glad, putting their hands on each other and feeling each other's heart beating. Kelly crosses the room and presses against the iron railing and she looks down. The two are in the pool, up to their chests and holding each other close. And Kelly thinks: that girl down there never wonders what he's thinking. She can feel free to laugh and do something without giving it a moment's consideration because there's never anything to wonder about, anything to worry her. She assumes she knows what's in his head. And maybe he actually says it. I love you, my baby, my sweetheart. That's part of her stupidity. He says something and she thinks it's so. But that's better than the alternative, isn't it? Even if what he says is a lie, if he says it, she can just be with him and do things and if it's all lies anyway, at least she can draw a breath without wondering how and why.

Kelly turns away from the balcony and takes a few small steps into the room and she has not yet driven to the courthouse and she has not yet phoned Drew and asked for him to come outside, to come outside to her, she has not yet done this, though it is in her mind to do it, and she is sitting at night on her deck with a pretty good Scotch, just two fingers and no more tonight, and Michael is sitting next to her and he is probably thinking about something other than sitting on the deck with her, or maybe thinking about how sitting on the deck with her is this utterly neutral thing, maybe thinking how there could have been a certain widely-longed-for strong feeling in his life and he either can't figure out what it was supposed to be or he knows, abstractly, what it is and what you call it, but out of his deep sense of personal integrity he will never speak of it overtly if he's not sure he feels it, while her own sense of integrity will never let her ask about it overtly if she's not already certain that it is so: she learned that much long ago, from another man, a man who, after all, upon due consideration, upon weighing everything even after waiting to see how his daughters turned out, simply preferred to be dead.

This is not good, Kelly thinks. This thinking is not good. I don't know a way to draw a breath around my own husband without wondering how and why. So she rises and goes into the house and pours two more fingers of Scotch and she comes back out onto the deck and she sits down, and it is not clear whether Michael even knew she was gone.

"I'm sorry," she says.

There is one beat, and then another, just long enough for her to think that she was right, that he does not even know whether she is there or not there, but on the third beat, Michael turns to her. "What about?" he says.

Kelly feels a twist of something she has to admit is disappointment. It would be easier if he could clearly be one thing or another about her. "I got up and didn't ask if you needed something."

"That's okay."

"What do you need?" Kelly says.

He doesn't reply.

"I'm asking it now."

He looks away. "Nothing. I'm fine."

"Good."

They are both silent for a time.

And then she says, "Work?"

"What?"

"Are you thinking about work?"

"No." And he says no more.

She stares into the darkness hovering beyond their backyard.

And after what feels to Kelly like a very long while, Michael says, "Sorry."

"Yes?" she says.

"Work. Yes. Some of that," he says.

Her mind is processing very slowly now, and it must show.

"Your question," he says. "Yes of course I was thinking about work. Aren't I always?"

"I suppose."

"But just not at that moment. The moment you asked."

She nods, though it is a gesture that she feels as remote from as if she were watching across the room, at a party for lawyers, as one stranger nods to another stranger.

"At that particular moment," Michael says, "I was trying to figure out if I need to bite the bullet and have the boat engine rebuilt."

She turns away from him. She sips her Scotch. She knows she is looking for a sign. She is waiting for her husband to say something that will make it impossible for her to do this thing she feels she is on the verge of doing. It doesn't have to be much. She has always hoarded away little scraps of seemingly tender things from him. Just a little something is all she needs. Soon.

But she's afraid he will fall silent now, and that will be that. She's driven to keep the sounds going, and so she hears herself say, "Engines need rebuilding." This sounds ridiculous to her. It *is* ridiculous. She has reached the tipping point with her Scotch way too soon.

But she sips a bit more. Burn, baby, burn. She almost says that aloud, almost addresses the Scotch going down her throat. She clenches her lips shut. She finds a point of light across the bayou and focuses on that. The light on someone's back porch. What are they doing inside? Arguing? Having sex? Sitting in a room together not saying a word?

"I get it," Michael says.

She turns to him. She doesn't understand what he gets.

"Okay," he says. "I'll make an appointment. But I'm fine. I'm in the pink."

"In the pink?"

"You and your impromptu metaphors."

"Have you gone mad, Michael?"

"I was just deciding you hadn't."

"Me?"

"Yes."

"But I have gone mad," she says.

"That thing about rebuilding engines," he says. "Sometimes I struggle when you get metaphorical."

"Ah, that. I'm also a little drunk."

"Then let's just forget it."

"What did you . . ."

"Nothing," he says. "I thought you were talking about the EKG. Dr. Neff suggested it. You lobbied for it. A few weeks ago."

"Drunk." Kelly lifts her glass at him. "Just drunk. Get the test or not. I'm sure 'in the pink' means something sexual, by the way. Sex for men. Speaking of metaphors."

"He said it was just routine. I'm of a certain age."

"Me too."

"We both are."

"I need to rebuild my engine," Kelly says.

And Michael shrugs and turns away.

Can something that will drastically change a life be decided like this? As stupidly as this? She puts her glass down on the deck beside her, several sips of Scotch left in it. She is, in fact, not drunk. Not at all. She and Michael have always talked like this. It's how they talk. Whatever she does, it's because of all of it.

And she lays her head back on the deck chair, and she closes her eyes, and she knows Michael will stay quiet now till one or the other of them rises and says it's time to sleep. And in this silence, and with the thing she must decide, she slides back only a few days, she lets the curtain fall on the first act of *Jesus Christ Superstar* and Judas has just sung that he won't be damned for all time and Michael has gone straight to his cell phone for something he's been thinking about for the whole first act, and Kelly rises and creeps up the aisle with the crowd and out into the Saenger's new crimson and gold lobby. This is the night of the Saenger's reopening and she stops beneath the skylight, and she looks up, and it seems small, it seems too small to have bothered.

"Only the janitors will see the stars through that," Drew says.

This third time she recognizes his voice at once, and she does not look at him, she keeps her face lifted to the skylight, which, it's true, shows nothing of the sky beyond because of the glare of lobby lights. She completes his thought. "After they're done and it's dark inside."

Kelly and Drew stare at the skylight for a few moments more, and then they lower their faces, aware of the synchronicity, and they turn to each other.

She holds back her smile. "Will you say it or should I?"

"I'll do it," he says.

But he doesn't.

"Well?" she says.

"We have to stop meeting like this."

Now she smiles, and so does he. He knew. "We do move in the same tight little world," she says.

"Yes." Drew lifts his face back to the skylight as he says, "Do you know why I hesitated?"

"No."

He continues to gaze upwards, as if he can't look her in the eyes for this. "I don't want to stop meeting like this."

What he says strikes her as something that she just felt as well, but would not have found words for.

He's looking at her now.

She has the impulse to do what she so often does with Michael when they talk, and what she has done with Drew in every conversation they've ever had: lightly twist and weave the small-talk. Banter über alles. And even though these words he has just spoken have followed that same pattern, his voice has gone soft and serious and he has averted his eyes as he's said them. He means what he says, and she feels the same way. And his eyes are steady on hers and her eyes are steady on his, and she leans ever so slightly toward him, and she lowers her voice as much as she can and still be heard over the babble of the intermission crowd—enough that he can hear the same earnestness that she has just heard—and she says, "If we stop, we'll just have to find another way."

He nods once at this. And then his eyes soften and narrow and unnarrow, and she senses from them that something has passed through him, and she knows to say, "Are you okay?"

"Why would you say that?" His literal words voice surprise but nothing about his body changes to express such a feeling.

"I don't know," Kelly says, and for the moment she doesn't.

He smiles a small, quick smile that vanishes at once. "Did you like the first act?"

Is he just changing the subject, intending no ambiguity, telling her indirectly to mind her own business, or is he still playing with the words, actually talking about the two of them, their own first act, and how they've been running into each other and how she now can even tell when he's troubled? "I have a feeling it's going to end badly," she says.

He takes this in. Makes a decision. "We're talking about the play?" he says.

"I don't know. Are we?"

"I'm not doing all that great," he says. "Since you asked."

"I'm sorry," she says.

"I didn't know it showed so clearly."

"I'm not sure it does."

"Only to you," he says, and his voice has gone soft enough that Kelly can barely hear him as a loud-talking couple passes by, speaking of chocolates.

"I didn't mean to intrude," she says.

"Not at all."

"This isn't a great place to talk."

"No."

"And our spouses are waiting," she says. And from the faint pull at the corners of his mouth Kelly knows that the trouble is with his wife.

Drew says, "The principal in my firm is a bene-factor of the theater."

She hears this as a preamble of an excuse for telling her that his wife isn't with him. But he pauses ever

so slightly before the hard part and Kelly finds herself
intervening. "Look," she says. "If the not-great thing
can benefit from a woman's advice, give me a call. We
can have coffee."

Drew's hand comes to her, touches her on the
forearm. "Do you mean that?"

"Of course."

"This is going to sound odd." But he says no more
for a moment.

"The silence?" she says.

He huffs a soft, self-deprecating laugh. "I'm working up my courage."

"I'll wait."

"Okay. I'd already thought . . . and this is the odd
part, for as briefly and accidentally as we've know each
other . . . It had already occurred to me that you'd be
someone I could actually talk to. Talk seriously."

Kelly finds herself having to wait for enough
breath to answer this, even as her mind rushes to first
acts and bad endings, even as she wants to take this
hand of his that still lingers on her arm and entwine
her fingers in his. But she simply says, "I think it's time
to exchange cell phone numbers."

~

And as Kelly stands in the center of Room 303 following memories within memories, Michael and Laurie are
arriving at the veranda of the plantation house. They
stop at its very edge. They have not spoken since they
left the berm of the levee. They have walked arm-in-
arm under the trees, and Laurie has connected Michael's
deep and—she is learning—characteristic silence with
his old-school romanticism. And that's okay, that's okay
for now and in this context; she is charmed by it. And
he is grateful for her silence. He is trying hard to stay
in the moment, trying to follow no memory at all but
simply be here with this beautiful young woman who
seems quite comfortable with him just as he is.

 The two of them linger at the edge of the veranda
and watch the chatting, drinking, posturing, period-
costumed twenty-first century lawyers and bankers
and doctors and real estate agents and small-business
owners. This is Laurie's event and Michael waits for
her to take the lead. And Laurie is considering this
dress-up fantasy thing she has chosen for the two of
them on the weekend when they will, with conscious
forethought and planning, do the deed for the first
time. Has she ever had sex like that before? Duh. No.
It's always been impulsive and impromptu. And she likes
it that way. Absolutely. But this way, it's as if the doing

of it will actually establish a very important connection between them: and it *is* important, she feels. It is. They are not just doin' it tonight. They are making love. She gets that, she is cool with that, OMFG, this could be something very big for her.

And she can make it her own. She moves her hand from the crook of his arm and she takes his hand and she entwines their fingers and she says, "I just got this great idea."

She waits, as if for a reaction, though she knows him enough to understand that the patient look he is giving her is all she will get. He is so cute sometimes.

"You've been very sweet," she says. "About the dress-up."

And in this dramatic pause she reaches up and puts her hand on his sweetly oft-straightened tie and she twists one end up.

Michael reflexively puts his own hand on the tie, thinking that she is straightening it and preferring to do that himself. He realizes what she has done instead.

She says, "But let's go now. I'm sorry I got this all mixed up. Let's go to our little cottage and make love right now, my romantic darling."

He looks steadily into her eyes as he fills with a warmth like the hit of a good Scotch. This is just what he needs to do right now. Just so.

Laurie waits for him, but in spite of the spin she's been applying to his silences, this one unsettles her. She says, "Romantic you, impulsive me. We can have it both ways, yes?"

Michael offers his arm and she takes it quickly and holds on tightly, and as they move away from the veranda, she says, "One thing, though. Turn off your cell phone."

And he stops at once and takes out his phone and he turns it off before her very eyes.

~

And Kelly makes her legs move, though they are very heavy. She tries to break free of the current that's carrying her. She moves from the center of the room, past the foot of the bed, and she stops in the space bound by three doors: to the bathroom, to the closet, to the corridor outside. And she is sitting at a table at Artissimo, near the red piano in the window, and Drew is across from her and they have been eating salad together and they have been talking small and they are near the theater where they met for the third time and they are very public here, in this tightly bound city where they live with their respective spouses, and they have done this because it is, of course, absolutely okay, anyone can see them because nothing is going on but an older woman meeting a younger male acquaintance to give some big-sisterly advice. But the two of them know, while there are people nearby, to talk small, and all the words they said in the restaurant on that day have vanished from Kelly now—except her saying to him, "You ordered a salad" and him saying to her, "Yes I did," and her saying, "Without steak or chicken in it," and him saying, "Certainly not," and her saying, laughing, "What kind of man are you?" and him saying, with a gravity and a look that are intended to remind them both of why they are here, "I have recently been asked that question"—and that was the thing, of course, the recent events in his life, and Kelly and Drew knew not to speak of it in the restaurant, they knew that they would not say a word even though it was the reason he called her the week after the Saenger and said, "Did you mean it, that I could talk with you?" and she said, "Yes, I meant it," and he suggested lunch and they came here and of course as soon as they got here it was clear that he couldn't talk about anything important because others could hear.

But then they finish their lunch and he pays and she insists on splitting the bill and he lets her do that and they do it in a very public way, lofting their two credit cards as if they are toasting with wine, and they go out the door, and without a word they begin to walk south on Palafox. Begin to stroll. Half an arm's length between them. Chaste. Obviously innocent. And they end up at the end of Palafox on a bench looking out at Pensacola Bay and there is still space between them.

"If you've changed your mind," Kelly says.

And he knows instantly what she means. "Not at all. I'm grateful for the chance to talk to you. It was the restaurant."

"Of course," she says. "But on the walk too."

"It was simply nice walking with you."

"It was."

"I didn't want to spoil it," he says.

"What kind of man are you?" she says, laughing again, but very softly.

He shrugs. "Inadequate," he says.

At this, Kelly wants to put her arms around him. She consciously holds very still, waits for more, but knowing already that the time will come when she will take him in her arms and help him make right whatever this is, knowing he will tell her. And she tries to hold still in this familiar room she's come to, and all the doors lead nowhere: the bathroom, the closet, an empty corridor, off a faux balcony. What should she have understood in those first moments with Drew Singleton? What should she have heard in what he said that would have told her to stand up and shake his hand and wish him well, that would have let her walk away and preserve what she had—at least that much—let her at least keep whatever she had.

After a very slight pause as he looks far out at the bay, no doubt contemplating his inadequacies, Drew suddenly does a little head snap and says, "Jeez. Listen to me. What a way to start this. I didn't ask you to lunch so I can wallow in self-pity or fish for compliments."

How could she have possibly walked away when he instantly co-opted any actionable fear she might be smart enough to have?

"You can say anything you want in any way you feel it," Kelly says to Drew. "I'll understand."

His eyes restlessly search her face as she speaks these words.

"Be yourself," she says.

Drew grasps her hand and squeezes it and she squeezes back and then he drops it at once. More reassurance for her to go on.

And he talks to Kelly of his wife. Of how he loves his wife. Of how she loves him. Of how, until she met him, she'd always been with men who were abusive in some way or other. Of how grateful she was to be with a man like him at last. But how she always seems to need more and how that's getting worse. She draws other men to her and needs to please them and Drew is certain—almost certain—almost certain but reluctant to consider anything else—he feels he is certain that she does not act in any private way on this need for attention, this need for constant reassurance.

At this point Kelly says, "I'm sure you tell her . . ."

"I tell her all the time," he says. "I wear my heart on my sleeve."

And Kelly initiates a touch. She takes his hand, and they are still holding hands as he says, "I let her know every day that I love her." Kelly squeezes his hand tightly, and she feels a welling-up in her chest, her throat, and she tries not to let it press tears from her eyes.

"But what I give her is not enough," he says. "And I think the very fact that I tell her—that I am the kind of man who will tell her—is the very thing that makes me inadequate."

And Kelly knows now, having moved back into the middle of Room 303, knows only after it is far too late, that if she were to be seduced, if she were to be persuaded to destroy her own life, this was the way for a man to do it.

And Drew squares around to face Kelly on the bench by the bay, as they work themselves up to an affair, and he takes her other hand in his and he lifts them both and he says, "Why are so many women

drawn to emotionally unavailable men, even as they
ask for openness and vulnerability?"

Kelly has no answer. As this man lifts her hands, she
can only think that her own life may be a testament to that
very problem. She has no answer. But she wants that
to change.

Drew says, "I saved her. She's always said that. But
I can't save myself."

Kelly finds herself standing before the night table.
The lovely pale-blue square, the mosaic of PERCOCET.
How did she not understand what was happening with
this man? What should she should have figured out
right away? His avowed inadequacy? His declaration
of it made her first want to hold him. But he didn't
really feel inadequate. He quickly made that simply be
about his declarations of love for his wife. He never
felt inadequate at all. He felt righteous. How did Kelly
miss that? And there was something important left
out of his perplexity over who's attracted to whom.
Why was he himself drawn to the woman he married,
knowing that she always fell for bad guys? Was it really
love he felt? Did he really think he could save her?
The thing about being on a white horse—and staying
quixotically on it—is that you yourself are unavailable up there. But she can't think it through now. It's
too late. She and this man drove fast on I-10 toward

the Alabama State line and as soon as they were out
of Pensacola they checked into the first motel they
came to, and the room smelled of concrete and carpet
cleaner, and they had sex and a dozen times he said he
loved her—it was foreplay talk, it was the pounding
talk, it was orgasm talk—and they came back to this
motel twice more, as if it were romantic, as if a cheap
interstate motel was something romantically their own
and the smell of carpet cleaner would never be the
same again, and then on the third time, after the sex,
he said that we all go through life loving and loving,
finding many people we love, and he loved her but he
loved his wife as well—which he'd been clear about
from the start—and he and Kelly had to face the bit-
tersweet reality that they couldn't really go on but
she was always going to be a perfect, self-contained
thing in his life and he hoped he would be that for
her. And that was that. And if she had not been an
absolute fool, if somehow the bullshit line he fed her
had actually been true in their case—in some universe,
between two specific people, it might well be true, she
supposed—then maybe she could indeed have put a
few beautiful memories away and kept them to herself,
but for her and for this particular man, it was a lie, it
was all a terrible lie, and it was done, and it was anything but beautiful, and worse, she had changed inside

and she could not face Michael by simply saying to herself *Oh well, fuck and learn.* She had not understood the fragile balancing act that was her life, and once she fell, she could not imagine a way to fly back up to that thin, hard wire above her. She could not imagine. She puts her forefinger on the night table and she draws it down through the square of pills, tumbling them apart.

She wanted so badly for it to have been good, for the words to be true and the touching to be true, even if for a few moments. Her body longed for that, and her body longs for that now, she feels a terrible scrabbling warmth come over her and she pulls at her little black dress, pulls at it from just below her hips, she pulls it up and off her and she unclasps her bra and sloughs it off and she slides her panties down her legs and steps from them and she is naked. She is as naked as she feels inside. She sat on the side of this bed only a few months ago and she told Michael what she had done. She could not bear to continue to sleep next to him and wake next to him and she could not bear to admire the churn and crackle of his mind and she could not bear his silences with that interstate motel room a secret. Because it happened, because it existed, because the fact of it went to bed with her and woke with her and it listened with her and it longed with her, and she had to put it outside of herself no matter what.

So she sat on this bed, and he was standing between her and the French windows, and the two of them had just arrived from dinner at Galatoire's, and she told him there was something she had to say and he squares around to face her and she says there is this terrible stupid thing she has done, and she tells him, and he keeps his eyes steady on her as she speaks, even as she tells it all, tells him the whole secret, and his face does not change, just as it does not change whenever she needs to know if he loves her, and she understands what is happening, she understands, and it spreads in her as a slow undulation of intense heat, and he says, "So it's done?" and his voice is flat, even as it clarifies—"Our marriage?"—and his eyes show nothing and the nothing of them suddenly quickens the heat in her, backdrafts words into her head and an impulse into her hands, she could fly at him and claw at him and cry out at him now, but she won't, she was the one in the motel room, that was her, she did this, but she is wildly angry at him even so and she can't say *No it's not done* and she can't say *Yes it is*. She says, "Is it?" and it's the right thing to say because if he says *Please darling no it can't be, it's over with you and this man isn't it? I can forgive you if you only say you want to stay with me*: if he says that, then it will be the same as saying *I love you* and she can hold on to those words forever and everything will be all right, everything will be better than it's ever been. But he says nothing. He turns his back abruptly on her and he moves to the French windows and he stands there, and from beyond him, from across the rooftops of the Quarter, from beside the river, comes the cry of a train. And after a long moment, and very low, so low she can only barely hear him, he says, "It always surprises me to hear a train whistle in the Quarter." And she says nothing. And he says nothing more. The flames have flared and died and she waits for whatever is next, and he is not moving, and she lowers her face, unable even to look at the back of him now, and she waits. Until, at last, she senses him turn. And she looks into his face. And it is blank. It is utterly blank. And she knows it's done.

And unaware of anything but the end of her marriage playing once more in her head, Kelly has moved now to the French windows, has pressed herself against the balustrade, and she looks out onto the moonlit rooftops, but she does not see them, all she sees is Michael's face, impassive, and even that is fading from her mind, and it is leaving nothing behind, and she is utterly unaware of what is below her: in the pool, the young couple in their improvised swimsuits standing up to their chests in water, facing each other, his hands around her waist, her hands on

his shoulders, and they have stopped joking about
what they are doing and they are quiet and looking
at each other and smelling the chlorine of the pool
and the young woman is thinking that the smell of
chlorine will never be the same again and she lifts
her face to the moon overhead, and though it is not
yet full, it is very bright, and her eyes drift from the
moon and she sees a woman standing in her open
French windows three floors above them, and the
woman is naked—she is slim and beautiful and she
is utterly naked—and the young woman lowers her
face to her lover and she motions upward with her
chin and they both look at the naked woman in the
French windows and they smile, and the young man
is thus moved to bring his hands up his lover's back
to the hooks on her bra and he undoes them and she
lets him do this, she draws her arms forward and she
takes the bra and she drops it away from her onto the
surface of the pool, and she and the young man press
their bodies together and they kiss, even as Kelly turns
and vanishes into her room.

~

And Michael and Laurie move through the moonlight
between the plantation house and their cottage, and

her hand is on his arm, and she is setting the pace. A
slow pace. She is relishing this walk to their bed, and
Michael is keenly aware that the phone on his hip
won't ring now, that this issue will remain unresolved
until tomorrow at the very least. He puts his hand on
Laurie's in the crook of his arm and he tries hard to
remain in this moment, with this new woman. But
instead, he stands before Kelly in the hotel room they
know so well and she says, "Michael," and she rarely
uses his name to address him, and she says, "Can we
talk?" and with that opening to what she wants to say,
he figures he has once again fallen short somehow,
probably from his preoccupied mind—and admittedly,
even as they have checked into what they think of as
their room, in their hotel, in their city, for a long weekend, he has been thinking mostly about a retired Navy
captain DUI he's trying to keep out of jail and get
into rehab, and he has no doubt that he has, in effect,
ignored Kelly since about the Louisiana border—so he
squares around before her and clears his mind and he
waits for her typically vague indictment. She is sitting
on the bed, and even after he has demonstrably given
her his full attention, she hesitates to speak, and he
feels uncomfortable standing over her when there is
apparently some sort of issue to deal with, and if she's
not going to rise to him, then he should probably sit

down beside her on the bed. But before he can, she starts to talk.

And in the moonlit dark full of the smell of sugar cane smoke, heading to his bed with this young woman beside him, Michael struggles to stop this memory. He does not want these words in his head. But they happen. As he remembers them. Stripped down. And when they were spoken, he felt very little as he heard them, as he tried to comprehend them. And when he found things to say in return, he heard his own voice as if it was someone else speaking.

"I've been sleeping with a man," Kelly says.

At first he has no words at all, not even in this other voice.

"It's over," she says.

"How long?" he says.

"For a month."

"Over for a month?"

"It lasted for a month. It's over now. For a few weeks."

"Why did it end?" And he realizes how odd this question is, preceding the more obvious *why did it start*.

"He stopped loving me," she says.

He takes this in. "And if his feelings hadn't changed?"

"I don't know."

"Why are you telling me?"

Then no words for a time. And then her voice again. "I find it's not so simple just to resume."

Then no words.

And then he says, "So it's done?" And he hears the ambiguity. Though she has already implied that the affair is done. But he could still be asking about that. He isn't. She has slept with another man and she has stopped because he has stopped loving her. She is not answering. He clarifies. "Our marriage?" he says.

She does not speak, and he feels himself catching up to all this. Those last two words came directly from his own mouth.

She says, "Is it?"

And he better turn his back now and move away because he knows already what is next, and that would be as difficult for him to face as the thing he has just faced: his eyes are growing thick with incipient tears. He is a wretched fool of a worthless child lost in the woods and about to cry. He turns his back to her and he walks to the open French windows and he clenches his eyes shut to stop the tears without touching them, without giving her the slightest clue as to what he's doing. Sightless, he hears a train whistle—one of the working trains rolling heavily along the edge of the city, out by the river. He says, "It always surprises me to hear a train whistle in the middle of New Orleans," and he has lost touch with his own voice again and he is losing touch with his own feelings again, as well, for he finds he can straighten and take a breath and set himself, and he will do what he needs to do. He allows himself a quick, heavy palming of his eyes so there will be no trace of any tear, and he turns to his wife, who, he is relieved to see, is staring not at him but at the floor. She seems to sense him watching. She lifts her eyes, and she looks at him, and her face is utterly blank. This always sweetly animated face has no trace of a feeling on it—in this extraordinary circumstance, there is no affect at all—and he knows the answer to the question. But he is all right, he is staying strong now: he imagines she needs him to be strong now, so that she can do what she needs to do.

And she says, "Yes. It's done."

"What is it?" This is Laurie's voice. Michael looks at her. They have stopped moving.

Her upturned face is blanched white in this light, and she seems young, so very young. But made alabaster by the moon, made into an ancient statue of a very young woman, she seems timeless, as well, grown already old in some distant past. And to this sense of her, Michael finds he can speak the thing in his mind.

"What did I miss?" he says.

She knows at once he's speaking of Kelly. "That she was cheating on you," Laurie says.

But that's not what he's trying to understand, and he can think of nothing more to ask.

"Did you ever cheat on her?" she says.

"No," he says.

"Were you ever tempted?"

"Abstractly. A time or two. But only in the abstract."

Laurie laughs, though it is a low, soft-edged laugh. "See," she says. "This is also *Men*. Or it once was. Here's a little secret, my darling. Some of us miss you old-fashioned guys. I'm a lucky girl."

Now she has stopped being a statue. Her dark eyes are intensely alive in the midst of her moon-cold face. And she no longer seems young in any way. He takes her in his arms and kisses her and the kiss goes on and then it turns into a gradually diminishing flutter of pecks and lip-pluckings and finally it ends.

They pull back slightly and they look each other in the eyes. And Laurie says, "I hope you realize that I'm falling madly in love with you."

~

On this night, as Michael hears an overt declaration of love from a new woman and as Kelly stands naked in the middle of her hotel room near her Scotch and her pills, as they both continue to churn with the past that brought them to this present moment, neither will turn to those strangely muted weeks following Kelly's confession. Michael moved into the Crowne Plaza, covering the desk with his papers and neatly lining up his empty two-a-night mini whiskey bottles on the TV cabinet, and Kelly often stood in the center of rooms for long stretches of time, listening to the ticking of her house or the humming of her refrigerator or the bratting of a motor boat passing on the bayou. When the two of them spoke, it was to deal with the details of the divorce, and they were sad and calm and quiet and business-like and mutually, wearily agreeable over assets.

One Sunday afternoon in the midst of the process, as Michael returned to the house to clean out his office downstairs, Kelly retreated to her office next to the master bedroom upstairs. Her office. She looks around. She has always worked. But Michael made it possible for her to work hard and not worry about making money. On the wall are photos of her with charity bigwigs and politicians. And framed thank-you letters. Make-A-Wish and the homeless. Habitat for Humanity and the symphony. The four causes she worked for over the years. Too many causes, perhaps. She was too restless. She should have stayed with one. But they all said thank you. And there were times—especially away from the offices, away from the fundraisers—at the hospitals and the shelters, at the building sites and the dressing rooms—there were times when they even said *we love you*. She thinks: how pathetic I have been.

She rises up and goes out of her office and into the bedroom and she closes the door and she locks it and she lies down on the bed and she begins to do the silent little number-mantra she's used over the years to clear her head and sleep. Oh three oh six eight four. Oh three oh six eight four. Keep those imageless numbers sounding loudly in her head, and the image-laden, free-associating thoughts—the sleep killers—don't have a chance to enter into her. But she sits up abruptly now. The numbers became simple sounds over the years, but the source of them lurches back into her now: March 6, 1984. Mardi Gras. The day she met Michael. She lies back down. She whispers softly to herself, "Oh shit." She will keep the house but she will lose her sleep aid.

But she soon sleeps anyway. And she wakes. And she has no idea how long it has been. It feels like a long time. She assumes it's been a long time. Her head feels pumped full of something hot and gaseous. She has a bitter taste in her mouth. She goes out of the bedroom and along the hall and down the stairs, and as she takes the last step into the foyer, Michael emerges from the hallway to his office. They both stop abruptly. It feels to her like the dark, alternate-universe equivalent to her stepping from the preparation room before her wedding, heading off to pee, and there he was. Out of place. Wanted and not wanted.

"You're still here," she says.

"I'm empty handed," he says. "But it's all sorted. I'll have someone come and move the things."

"I lost track of time is all. I slept."

"Good," he says. Softly.

They stand where they are. They don't move.

"I was just leaving." he says.

"All right."

"My office . . ." he begins, but he doesn't finish the thought. He tries to decide whether to speak the thing that struck him a short time ago, as he was preparing to leave his life in this house, in this marriage. Ever since that terrible early evening in the Quarter, he has said nothing, asked nothing, about what happened to make her go to another man. It happened. She sought it. The other man ended it. The last thing Michael wants to do—it would be impossible for him—is to do anything to persuade her to stay with him. It's a thing the woman who is his wife either wants for herself or she doesn't. His life is built on advocacy, but he realized as soon as he forced back those initial tears that for him there can be absolutely no advocacy in this circumstance. She has to want him freely, with no persuasion, or she doesn't want him at all. Prima facie. And what he would say right now could be misconstrued as a kind of persuasion, and that's why he is hesitating. But he wants her to know. "My office," he says, "seems cleaner than it should be."

"I haven't touched a thing," Kelly says

"I'm not suggesting you have." His hands flare open before him. And of all things to think about right now, it strikes him that the gesture he just made has some deeply instinctive link back to the caves, a show of having no weapon. He's thinking a little crazy now. He drags his mind back to this thought he had while emptying his office. "I was just realizing," he says. He stops again. What has he realized? "I just realized that I never spent as much time working at home as I thought I would." He should never have begun this. He knew not to say anything, he knew just to let her go, but now he's sounding crazy, as well.

But Kelly knows what he's trying to say. "That was never an issue," she says. And if she has some inclination—some—yes, of course she has some—if she is in any way open at last to saying the things she could not say before, now that she isn't asking for them anymore, now that she has herself burned down this life they'd made together, now that it makes no difference anyway if he actually loves her enough to say so freely and explicitly—if she has any impulse to explain how all of the unspoken things became a deep river-current that eventually swept her away, it vanishes abruptly with this cluelessness of his. She had sex with a man she hardly knew and in doing so destroyed the inner life of this marriage, and he thinks it might be about where he did his paperwork?

He's not answering.

"Do you think it was about that?" she says, and she sounds to herself as if she's speaking while choking.

"I don't know."

"You don't know?"

"How am I supposed to know?"

"How?" Her throat has suddenly cleared and her voice rings loud around them both.

He keeps his own voice low but firm. "You had an affair and it's the last thing in the world I expected and you said the marriage is over and we're not talking about it and I'm fine with that but . . ."

"I'm sure you're fine with that."

"But I can't be blamed . . ."

"Of course we're not talking." And Kelly is shouting.

And Michael wants to shout but he doesn't, he finds the same control of his voice he finds in a courtroom, and he says, "I can't be blamed if I'm wrong about some of the things . . ."

"So blame *me*," she cries. "I deserve it. If you can't love me then at least hate me."

And he doesn't say a word. He moves past her and he opens the front door and he goes out and he doesn't think to close the door and she watches for a moment as he goes down the walk, and then she turns her face away from him and her hands were too slow, her hands wish now they'd clawed at his face as he passed, just to get him to do something in return, anything.

~

And Michael says nothing in response to Laurie's declaration of love. Not that there's a recoil in him. He simply does not hear it for what it is. For Michael, it is a woman's rhetoric. These are simply words. Easy currency for a woman. For him, she's here and he's here with her. That's so because they find things in each other they each seem legitimately to enjoy. They're going to their cottage and they will be naked together and they will join their bodies and they will unjoin them. They will fall asleep together. They will wake and they will rise in the morning. Good morning, how'd you sleep. Fine. They will eat breakfast in the restaurant that was once the living quarters for the post-war field workers. Are you enjoying yourself? Yes. And you? And now and then he will think about the retired Navy captain and also about Monday afternoon and jury selection for a pro-bono who will be tough to protect from bias. While Michael is with Laurie, he will think of no other woman in the same way that he is thinking of her. He will try to think of no other woman at all, particularly the woman at the center of a considerable pain in him. He will be open to the possibility of many more nights of joining and of sleeping and of waking with this woman he has just kissed. For him, that too is considerable. And his response to her rhetoric is to let his hand fall to the small of her back and to turn her and move them off toward the cottage. And for now, this gesture—particularly his hand in the small of her back—is sufficient for Laurie.

As they cross the last hundred yards of tarnished-silver ground to the cottage, Michael tries to stay focused on the present moment with this young woman, and it is true that the soft clinging of her, and the moon-shadow of pressure remaining on his lips from the kiss, and the imminence of their nakedness are beginning to rustle in his body. And her silence now. Her silence is part of this readying of his body and mind for the first night of full togetherness with a new woman. After a long while, after many years, it is made new. He fends off the past. There has already been too much of that. But the things he responds to in women in what feel to him like instinctive ways are running strong in him, things he has, however, learned from a multitude of memories that are too small individually and happened too long ago for him ever to recall.

His mother moving silently in the dark next to him, just that, along a street thick with the early heat of a Florida spring night and the smell of Confederate jasmine, porch lights lit, passing distantly, and his mother at his side keeping still, and he wakes and leaps from bed as blood flows from the ceiling, a moment ago from a deer hung for dressing but from the ceiling now, from the light fixture and into his bed and she takes him in her arms and his father's silhouette fills the doorway and Michael does not know that the man has moments ago put his hand roughly on her arm to prevent her going in to a boy who needs to be a man and she defied her husband this time, for once, and he warned her at least not to say anything, not to prattle on like usual, and she agreed to that so he would let go of her arm—though his hand had loosened already, it had not yet let go—and she did go in and Michael never knew any of this occurred outside his door as he pants heavily, as if his heart will stop, still making sounds that he knows shame the shadow in the doorway—that shame his father—and his mother comes to him and she holds him and then she leads him back to bed and she sits beside him and his heart slows and the blood is gone, the blood was never there, and it's all right, and he takes in her silence, he rests now in her silence, and he too has come to prefer this, from when he was very small, from the sharp sideways looks and abrupt shushings from his father to his mother when Michael was just beginning to gather the momentum of his own words, when he was hearing the rhythms and flow of his mother's voice in his own head, when he was open to imitating them, and she always fell silent when commanded, teaching Michael how to learn what's right and good, by yielding to this man, and she moves beside him along a street on a spring night and they are going somewhere together just the two of them and the air is sweet and he loves his mother and these memories are long vanished from Michael in all but the dark and the sweet rustle of a woman and the silence.

~

"I'm naked," Kelly says aloud. She crosses her arms over her chest and covers her nipples with her hands. How is it that I'm naked? This she says only in her head. She is standing in the middle of the floor at the foot of the bed. She looks around her. She does not find her clothes. She turns. The French windows are open. But no one can see. There are only moonlit rooftops and, in the distance, a *Marriott* and a *Sheraton* floating near each other in red neon with a gold speckling of their room lights below. She lowers her hands. But she wants to be clothed now. She moves along the bed and she sees her dress crumpled before the night table, as if she has already taken her Scotch and her pills and she has simply vanished, a dark rapture that has carried off her body and left her clothes behind.

She goes to her dress and picks it up and lifts it and lets it fall over her. She is unaware of the lick of its silk going down her body. She is very aware of the bottle and the pills, but she goes up onto the bed on her knees and she turns and sits, her back against the iron headboard. The wrought-iron bars press hard at her and she leans forward and twists around and uprights a pillow there. She straightens and leans back again. She understands the irony. She's protecting her body from this minor discomfort even as she intends to send that body to the grave. Tonight. Soon. But that will be just a larger-scale plumping of a pillow. Once she's there, the grave is painless. And living isn't. Living is full of pain now. More so now. Much more now. Now that she's destroyed her family. Sam loved having a family. Sam needs a family. She's let Sam down. Horribly. Forever. She's put a poisonous thing inside herself that's a far worse poison than a handful of pain pills because it preserves her consciousness, heightens her consciousness, keeps her awake forever to all that she's lost.

These are words in Kelly's head. She's talking it out in there abstractly, and she realizes that it's safer that way. She's reasoning a thing out that in fact lives beyond words. It lives in her limbs and her chest and her face and her loins. That's the terrible power of what she's done. There are no words to fix it. No words to properly describe it. But it was words withheld, it was words not spoken, it was silence that led her to this. "No." She says this aloud, into the room. Her voice is low but it feels as if she's just yelled. No need to yell. The point is, she says to herself in her head, it's never been about words. They're just signifiers. And the absence of words signifies too. She has never been loved. She has never been worthy of that.

She needs a drink.

But she doesn't take it yet.

The final afternoon when she and a man she hardly knew had sex in a cheap motel and she failed to measure up, when she failed to keep this man beside her no matter how often he said the words she always thought would fix her, that final afternoon they'd come to the motel separately. He'd suggested that. She didn't realize it, but she had already failed to measure up. He said he loved her a number of times that afternoon but it was already not true. It had never been true. He had suggested they come separately because he didn't want to have an awkward trip together afterwards. So she gets into her car and she drives out of the motel parking lot and onto I-10 and she heads east, back to Pensacola. Back to her house. And to what else? Back to what life? There are no words for that, either. She is rushing at 70 miles an hour along a highway toward nothing. And quite slowly, quite gently, she closes her eyes. She holds her eyes shut and looks at this darkness. She looks and she waits and she looks. She waits for what feels like a very long time, and then there is a vibration in her hands and a rough, deep pulsing sound fills the car, and she simply opens her eyes. She has drifted off the road—she expected that, surely—that's what she was seeking, of course—but the turnpike wake-up grooves have opened her eyes by reflex, and by reflex, by weary inertia, she keeps them open, and she guides the car back onto the highway. And she knows how stupid she is, how self-absorbed, to have endangered others.

She needs a drink.

Kelly turns to the night table, and she pours herself some Scotch. A couple of fingers, more or less. She doesn't want to lose her focus now from simple drunkenness and wake to another day when she has to start all this over again. It's better at night. It's better now. But she will begin with a little more Scotch. She lifts the glass from the table and sits back against the pillow—she is quite comfortable, actually—like those moments driving fast and smooth and blind, simply looking into the darkness within her own eyes.

She sips her Scotch. She closes her eyes. She touches her hair. She should have done her hair. Not long ago, when she was already as sad as this, she did her hair for herself, for her birthday. She sat like this with a Scotch, on the deck of their house. Of *her* house. He let the house go to her. He never said. He never said but she knew. She had defiled this place he'd built for them. He could have forced a sale to equally divide the asset, but he didn't. He wanted her to have it but he never said why. She knew it was a rebuke. And she let other assets go to him in compensation. He made the money. That was his mistress. She endured the long whiling of silence spent in her house as he made the money. She didn't want to move out of the house. She couldn't face that. She puts her hair up in a French twist for her birthday, and she puts on her makeup. She sits down at twilight and lets the dark come upon her. She thinks she hears the beating of wings, the slow beating of the wings of an egret flying past in the darkness. Do egrets fly in the dark? She can't imagine. And she thinks of the first hours she spent with her future husband. On the deck of her house and on the bed in Room 303, she thinks of the first hours of Kelly and Michael.

He rescued her. He took her to his room at the Olivier House. He did not hold her till she said he could and then it was to stop her trembling. To make her feel safe. She stopped trembling. She felt safe. And then they sat in the two chairs on either side of the French windows, and the last of the daylight was fading outside. They talked small and they laughed some and they kept the windows closed so they could hear each other, as the Mardi Gras din pressed into the room. And the small talk finally accumulated enough that they could feel they'd met properly, that they'd done enough to suggest doing a little bit more. In a mutual pause, Michael looks out the window and he says, "Do you think we should try again out there?"

"Yes," Kelly says.

"You sure it's okay? You've been through it."

Kelly smiles at this sweetly solicitous man. She says, "The operative word is *we*."

"Of course."

And so they go out. They move along Toulouse and turn onto Bourbon, and for the rest of the evening neither of them even gets a drink. They simply drift together in the crowd, at the edge a little faster but also content to nudge and wedge and stand and float in the density of bodies in the middle of the street, watching, apart together even in the midst of all this, holding hands, and as midnight nears, they squeeze out of the mass, onto the sidewalk, and a blues band is playing somewhere nearby and the two of them find a small square of sidewalk, barely enough to flare their elbows but a space of their own nonetheless, and the music is something Kelly can no longer remember but it is a fast song, an old New Orleans blues song that suffers the blues with a fast tempo, and Michael puts his hand in the small of her back and he is turning her to face him and that hand on her back comes up higher and her first thought is that he is about to kiss her, and she is ready for that, she raises her face to him, but his other hand has taken her hand now and he lifts it and she realizes he wants to dance, and he presses her to him and they move in tiny steps on their small circle of pavement and they dance a slow dance, as if this is the Stylistics playing, as if this is a dance at the American Legion Hall and they are slow-dancing to "Betcha By Golly Wow." Michael has taken her in his arms and is dancing with her and he is defying the crowd and the noise and the drunkenness and the band's insistence on being fast and loud. He has his own ideas about the two of them. And Kelly is happy in that moment. Kelly is very happy. And how could she have known? How could she have ever known? She will never again in her life feel as loved as she does before she even knows for sure she is in love, before she has even kissed her future husband for the first time.

And now this.

But for taking her in his arms and dancing slow with her in the middle of Mardi Gras, she will say good-bye to him, she will apologize for what she has done and for what she will do. And with that intention comes a resolution: if she hears his actual voice, if he answers the phone, she will simply say *I'm sorry* and she will hang up. Because she needs nothing from him. And she knows now what she must do.

She sets her empty glass on the night stand, careful to avoid the pills.

Her phone. Her purse. She rises from the bed, stands unsteadily. She cannot remember having her purse. She's afraid she left it somewhere out there in the dark. Perhaps by the river. She moves along the bed and she sees the purse on the floor near the foot of the bed.

She goes to it. She bends to it. She pushes her hand through the clutter of unidentifiable objects inside, looking for the phone, and her fingertips touch the fluted metal tube of her lipstick and for the briefest of moments she pauses with the thought that she will never look at herself in the mirror again, never put color on her lips, never run a brush through her hair, and in that moment she is sad for herself, as if she were some other woman, some other woman who has reached the end of what she can bear in this life and Kelly is sad for her, and her hand moves on and it finds the phone and she draws it out and she rises and she turns and she faces the open windows. Beyond, New Orleans is silent. Utterly silent. She opens the phone and dials Michael's cell.

~

And it does not make a sound. It is holstered and muted, attached to Michael's belt and lying in the heap of his trousers across the room from the bed where Michael and Laurie are making love, Laurie happy to have at last guided herself on top and Michael uncomfortable still about being on the bottom but getting over it, though his eyes are not on the woman he is connected to, unlike all the times he made love to Kelly through the years, all the times he watched her face while she was unaware, closing her own eyes as she always did, squeezing them shut and furrowing her brow as if listening to some distant voice she could barely hear but that was trying to tell her something important. Michael's own eyes with Laurie are shifted slightly away, looking at the blank expanse of the ceiling but without seeing what's before him, without quite being in his body or in this moment, and he does want that, he does want to be here, be here vividly with Laurie, but he finds—a little bit to his surprise—that his body is so imprinted with Kelly's that the difference of shape and texture and smell and sound of this new woman distances him from all this. Though not in any way that Laurie would notice. I will adjust, he thinks. And he closes his eyes. And Kelly is in him and they are in a dark room and she is making a sound beneath him like something hurts her bad or like something gives her great joy and she herself cannot tell them apart and so she has to cry out in a way such that no one listening could ever understand what she feels. She is a terrible, everlasting mystery, and though Michael cares what she is feeling, he knows he can never know, and he adjusts, he adjusts.

And as he listens to Kelly beneath him while Laurie cries out above him, the phone stops silently flashing, and it is never seen, buried as it is in Michael's clothes scattered before sex.

~

And very soon thereafter, Michael and Laurie have finished and both their bodies quake softly from all that, and she is lying beside him, and she curls against him and his arm goes around her, and she says, "Michael, Michael, you were . . ." and she pauses. She pauses to tease him but pauses also to find just the right words.

Michael waits, and he realizes, a little to his surprise, that he is indifferent to what might follow. He always wondered what Kelly thought of him in bed. More than wondered. He wanted very much for her to find him good at this. But he could never ask. If he asked and he got the answer he desired, he would never be able to take it as anything but a pretty lie. She had to say it on her own or it could never be said. But with Laurie, ready now to tell him of her own free will, he feels no welling of interest, no fear either. It is what it is.

"Stoically great," Laurie says.

He looks at her. He has no idea what that means.

Laurie lifts her free hand and puts the tip of her finger on the tip of his nose and gently pushes. "That's a compliment," she says.

He looks back to the ceiling. He pulls her close.

"Thank you," she says.

"For my stoicism?"

"For taking me seriously."

"Of course," he says.

"That's Michael. 'Of course', he says. That's my Michael."

He doesn't want to talk about who or what he is. But he knows Laurie is trying to be good to him. He gives her a little squeeze. A little thanks-but-let's-move-on squeeze.

She says, "You were so sad that day at the office when I realized I had to get closer to you. So sad. That was about your third trip to Mr. Bloom over the divorce."

"Can we stay in this moment? Just the two of us?" Michael says.

Laurie lifts her head. "Oh darling, of course. I'm sorry."

She nuzzles her head back into the hollow between his shoulder and chest.

He wants to be quiet now. He wants to be quiet for a long while. He wants to be by himself, to be honest. He wants to kiss her sweetly good night and then go somewhere else. He realizes this with a little inner flinch. But he knows he will stay with her. His rational mind is glad he has a woman now. But everything else about him feels spent. He feels he needs to be away from her for a little while in order to want her again. He wishes he felt otherwise. So he will stay. But he is glad there is a moment of silence, and another. He is glad Laurie is capable of being quiet.

"I'm sleepy," she says.

"Good," he says. "I am too."

"I have to say this first, though."

He does not reply but turns his head slightly in her direction. Let's get it over with.

She lifts her head from him, rises up on an elbow. "I said something outside. I need to adjust that."

He knows what she's referring to. For a moment he thinks things will be all right. He has prior evidence of her knack for knowing what he needs. He is relying on that now. He needs for her to pull back from what she said.

She straightens up fully now, squares around to face him. "I said I am falling madly in love with you."

She pauses. He waits.

"I got the verb tense wrong," she says. "Have fallen, my darling. I *have* fallen madly in love with you."

She waits for Michael to respond. He says nothing rather than what's in his head: I don't need this now.

"It feels so like we've done this right," she says.

She pauses again. She sees Michael as a man of words. Words are his business. She is a bit awed by all the lawyers and how they live by words. She needs to work this out in words now. And having thus far found Michael's reticence with her to be charmingly masculine, sexy even, she has no clue what's going on in him.

"Even us waiting to make love," she says. "How right was that?" She would like a nod—if not a word—of agreement from him at this point, at least about how they were right to go slow. But he's not giving it. And she suddenly thinks she understands what's making him hesitate. It's her image as a lightweight—and she's at fault, she knows, for nurturing that. That silliness at their second meeting, for instance. She loves him even more for having gotten past that, but she's afraid that he's afraid she's being superficial about her feelings. She says, "I don't use the word 'love' lightly, my darling. Don't worry."

He's looking at her but he's not speaking. The light is dim in the room. She needs to read his eyes closely and she can't. "I've almost never said it to a boyfriend," she says. "But you know me. I have to speak my heart when I feel something."

Michael, in fact, does not know this about her. He does not know what to say. He does not know what to do. He feels himself staring dumbly, and he thinks he does not know the first thing about women. Not a single thing.

Laurie, aware that she needs to make sure her voice does not falter, but utterly unaware of her own gesture, lays her arm laterally across her chest, covering one nipple with her forearm and one with her hand. She says, "Am I at risk here?"

"I don't know what risk you're talking about," Michael says, not argumentative but truly baffled.

"You don't?" Laurie says. "Really?"

He has no answer.

"Any verb tense will be okay," she says.

Nothing.

"The risk," Laurie says, very softly, loving this man and trusting him, running out of breath and needing to start again, her arm falling to her side. "The risk is you're not falling in love with me."

"I'm here. Isn't that enough?" Michael says, though taking care to match the softness of her voice. "We did this," he says.

"Please tell me what that means," Laurie says.

He tries to distance himself with the notion that he has no idea what she wants. But he knows that's not true. But knowing what she wants doesn't make it possible for him to give it to her.

"I need some help here, Michael. Tell me what you feel."

"Is it the word you need?" he says.

"I guess I do," she says.

And he says, "Love means never having to say I love you." Part of him truly believes this. But another part suddenly hears himself sounding like a bad country music song.

Laurie rises abruptly to her knees. "Are you fucking kidding me? Do you know how many people in this world have been fucked up from the start by somebody having that idea?"

He backs away from this. "I'm going to get some air," he says.

He rises from the bed, crosses the room, bends to his pants, pulls them on, his belt swinging heavily free, with his cell phone attached. As he reloops the belt, Laurie finally finds the voice to deal with his withdrawal.

"Michael," she says. He finishes cinching his belt, and then he turns to her.

She is still on her knees on the bed. "I need this," Laurie says. "People need this."

She is speaking softly again. Her need. People's needs. He is bare-chested. Her nakedness, her quietness, her need: he feels these like a pressure on his chest, like her body falling forward and pressing into him after they both finished, her body still there when they should be separating for a time, her body suddenly too warm, too wet, too much.

He bends, he picks up his shirt, he turns his back on her, puts the shirt on, buttoning hastily as he finds his shoes, slips them on. He has to get some air. He said that already.

He is moving through the dim rooms, and in contradiction to his sounder, wiser, lawyerly judgment, he thinks: I'm fucking this up with this sweet and beautiful young woman. He is pushing through the screen door of the cottage. To ward off an even worse culpability over Kelly, he denies this one now. She's a child. He's old enough to be her father. What did he expect.

He walks briskly a dozen paces away from the cottage and he stops. The moon is high. The smell of sugar cane smoke, of something sweet burnt down, is strong in the air. He shouldn't be blaming Laurie. If it's wrong with her, it's wrong. But what made it go wrong so abruptly? He stands very still beneath the moon, and just as abruptly, he is uneasy with himself in many ways. Many. But he would have trouble clearly articulating any of them. And he and Kelly enter the room they have made their own over the years, Room 303 at the Olivier House in the Quarter. They've had dinner at Galatoire's and she's been very quiet and of course he has appreciated that, of course he has assumed that things are very good between them because she is happy to be quiet with him, and he hangs up his suit coat and he crosses the room loosening his tie and she has drifted toward the bed. He opens the French windows.

"It's hot in here," he says. "Or maybe that's just the oysters backing up on me."

He looks out at the moon, perched brightly on the farthest rooftop.

He turns.

Kelly is sitting on the side of the bed. She looks up at him. "Michael," she says, and she stops.

He takes a step toward her, and he waits for a moment. Then he says, "What is it?"

She looks away. Her shoulders hunch a little. "It's just the oysters," she says.

He accepts this. He has cufflinks. He thinks to take them off.

"Was I pretty tonight?" she says.

"Of course," Michael says.

She falls silent again. He's not sure if he can move away to deal with his cufflinks now. There may be more.

And then she says, "There are things I need. Things I've always needed."

And Michael turns around beneath the moon at Oak Alley Plantation, even as he hears himself say to Kelly "What things do you need?" He faces the cottage where Laurie waits. And he stands before Kelly.

"Was I pretty tonight?" she says.

"Of course," he says.

"There are things I need," she says.

"What things do you need?" he says.

"I've been sleeping with a man," she says.

And he stops this now. His hand goes to his phone. He'll try once more to get through. He flips open the cell and he has a message. The number is hers. It couldn't have been long ago. He starts the message and puts the phone to his ear.

And Kelly's voice says, "It's me. With things unsaid between us—forever unsaid—I didn't want this all to end without my saying I'm sorry. I am. For this. For everything. You did the best you could. So did I . . . I hoped to hear a train tonight and just fade away with it down the river. But I know it's almost time now, and there's only silence . . . I love this room. Can you love a room? Or is that just a word? No. I love this room. I always have. Maybe I'll haunt it . . . And my darling, I love you too. I always have."

Michael redials her number and he knows what will happen but he has to try, he has to hold himself in suspension till at least he tries. Her phone rings and rings and rings and rings and rings and it rings and it clicks and her voice message begins and Michael snaps his phone shut. He sprints to the cottage and he slams through the screen door and the front door and he rushes toward the bedroom. Laurie has heard the violence of his entry and when Michael bursts into the room she has scrambled against the headboard. He sees her eyes wide and her hands flat hard against the mattress, pressing her backwards. "God no," he says. "It's not about you. I had a phone message. I think Kelly's trying to kill herself."

Laurie rises to her knees. "Oh, Michael."

"I have to go," he says, moving to the dresser. "I'm sorry."

"No," she says. "Do what you have to do."

He grabs his wallet and his keys and he turns back to Laurie.

"I'm sorry for everything," he says.

"Go," she says.

Michael nods and he rushes out of the room.

Laurie sinks back down, presses herself against the headboard once more. She closes her eyes hard, waits for the tears. She wants Kelly to live. But she knows that whatever happens, she has lost Michael.

~

And Michael roars down the perimeter road of the plantation, not thinking yet, and the intersection with Highway 18 looms ahead and he hits his brakes hard and he feels a flutter of fishtail in his car and he asserts his mind, realizing he can't help Kelly if he ends up in a ditch. He makes the full stop at 18. He has thought of a thing to do first. He opens his phone and scans through the phone directory and finds the number for the Olivier House. He dials the number even as he slides out onto the highway and accelerates, going as fast as he can and still control his car with one hand. He puts the phone to his ear and a woman's voice answers.

"Olivier House." A familiar voice.

"This is Michael Hays."

"Mr. Hays?"

"Yes. I need to speak to my wife."

"She's not here."

"Room 303," he says.

"She's not registered here, Mr. Hays."

Michael feels a slamming of brakes in him. Maybe he's wrong. No. She was talking about their room at the Olivier, clearly. He says, "It's Ramona, isn't it?"

"Yes."

"Ramona, I feel certain she's there."

"I know Mrs. Hays quite well," she says. "She's definitely not here."

"You're on nights," Michael says. "You simply haven't seen her. Room 303. Try 303."

And Ramona says, "Oh, I know who's in Room 303. It's not Mrs. Hays."

Michael just drives for a moment, just rushes in the dark past the stubbled cane fields white in the moonlight. He does have a shard of a doubt. He has to advocate here. For Kelly's sake, he has to act as if it's true. He says, "She's told you to say this, Ramona. But listen very carefully. I have good reason to believe she's harming herself. Right now. In your hotel."

There is a beat of silence on the other end. He wishes he could see this woman. He wishes he could watch her eyes. Is she hesitating because he's right? Or is she offended at being called a liar when she's not?

Ramona says, "I'm telling you she's not here."

"Please at least check on her," Michael says. "Please."

"On who, Mr. Hays?" Ramona says. "I have to go now. I have someone checking in."

And she's gone.

Michael snaps his phone shut and lays it on the seat next to him. He has to act as if she's lying. "Take your time, baby," he says aloud as he puts both hands on the wheel and leans into the wide, white column of light he's pushing before him. "Take your time." And he accelerates, he races as fast as he dare along the river.

~

And at the Olivier House front desk, Ramona stares at the phone. She is not a natural liar. She is a reluctant liar. She hates to lie. She hates it so much, she knows the count. Six. She has lied six times in the past minute and a half. But it's for a good cause. The husband was scary. Too intense. She could feel it over the phone. She could understand Mrs. Hays asking her to do this, to lie. And she needs to find something other than "Mrs. Hays" to call her. Would "Kelly" be too familiar? But even as she feels whatever is going on here is something sadly typical between a man and woman, Ramona, too, has a shard of doubt beginning to tumble through her head. A small shard, but a shard nonetheless.

She pushes back from the desk and rises. She turns and crosses to the double doors at the back of the entrance hall and she opens them and steps out. She pauses. She doesn't want to disturb Kelly. But if there is even a small chance that Mr. Hays is right, then she must. She moves on into the deep shadow of the loggia, the pool glowing ahead, and she emerges into the courtyard, focused now on making sure Kelly is all right. Vaguely aware, as she always is, of the thirty-foot ficus on the far side of the pool, a crazy overgrown thing, she turns to the staircase, utterly unaware of the young man and young woman from Room 107 in the middle of the pool, both of them naked, holding each other close. Their laughter, at their own paralyzed panic at nearly being caught, follows Ramona up the stairs.

She is oblivious to it. She's climbing the stairs quickly now, quickly, wanting to get this over with, wanting to put her own mind at ease. She emerges on the third floor and steps to the door of Room 303. She hesitates once more, but she must do this. She knocks. Too lightly, she knows. There's no response. She knocks harder. "Mrs. Hays," she says. "It's Ramona."

She hears nothing from within. She's hesitant. Kelly is getting some needed rest. Ramona's disturbing her at the say-so of a controlling man. But she decides to try again. And she hears her own mistake. "I'm sorry," she says through the door. "I mean . . . Kelly, isn't it? Kelly, it's Ramona."

Nothing. Ramona raises her hand again to the door. But she stops, unable to do a thing. She should just go. She should knock again. She should go.

And the door opens. It's Kelly.

Clearly she's been crying. Her eyes are wet. And they are trying to droop shut. She smells strongly of liquor. She deserves to get drunk in peace. Ramona has made a terrible mistake.

"What is it, Ramona?" Kelly says.

"I'm sorry to disturb you," she says, though she does have to ask, for the record. "Are you okay?"

"I've been crying," Kelly says. "I thought I'd finished. I wasn't. But I am now. I almost am."

"I didn't mean to bother you," Ramona says.

"I had to finish this first," Kelly says. "I don't know why."

"I'm very sorry."

"I'm going to go to sleep," Kelly says.

"It was your husband, is why," Ramona says. "He called."

"What did you tell him?"

"You're not here."

"Good."

"Have a nice long sleep," Ramona says.

"I will," Kelly says, so softly Ramona can barely hear. But then Kelly speaks up, her voice reassuringly firm. "You cry enough," Kelly says, "it all finally gets clear, you know?"

"Oh I do," Ramona says.

"I'm feeling calm," Kelly says.

"Good."

"Good night," Kelly says.

"Good night," Ramona says.

The door closes. Ramona gives the door a little nod and she goes.

~

Out in the night, Michael is pushing hard, and ahead he can see flashing red lights in the night sky, floating above the horizon, and beyond is a vast yellow glow. The lights are the Gramercy Bridge. The glow is the alumina refinery. He's still fifty miles from New Orleans. He will speed up, but he slows a little first and he reaches to his phone. He dials Kelly's cell. It rings and rings again and he does not know that Kelly, returning from the door after speaking with Ramona, stands before the phone as it rings a third time, and he does not know that her tears have ended and that she takes the phone into her hand and steps unsteadily to the French windows and that she throws the phone into the night. And neither of them knows that the phone falls and falls and rings once more as it falls, turning the faces of a naked young couple just in time to see a tiny splash of water at the far end of the pool.

~

And Michael drives fast and Michael tries not to think, tries just to keep focused on the road, the steering wheel, his lights out before him, and he is crossing the Gramercy Bridge with the bright yellow blare of the refinery beside him and its mountain peaks of alumina red mud and of gypsum waste and he is off the bridge and he slows for a stoplight, checking for traffic and cops, and he accelerates through and he's racing in the dark and the pine forests scroll past on both sides and she is touching him, she runs her hand down his chest in the dark, his Kelly, and she sighs, and he shakes off this memory and he realizes he has opened by instinct, by his own preemptive preference, to a moment when she was silent, when perhaps she wanted to speak when perhaps she wanted to say these things she needed to say and perhaps she touched his chest instead, having touched him enough already, needing now to add

words to the touching, needing this, but with him,
married to him, made silent by him, she was able only
to touch, and Michael grips the wheel harder and he
presses on and the interstate is ahead at last and he
follows a sign though it seems as if he's simply veering
into the woods and he follows this narrow way and
he follows and he follows and it's dark and he feels
the pulse of his heart in his ears and at last the woods
vanish and a bright-lit semi roars past him and Michael
slides into the near lane of I-10 and he can make real
time and he keeps sliding into the passing lane and he
accelerates rushing past the truck and on and on and
he has only the flare of his headlights before him and
the pulse of the white lines beneath him and he stays
mindless now he can stay mindless and the highway
rises and the median vanishes and beside him is a dark
void beyond a concrete rail he is in cypress treetops
and for a time the world becomes for him, below and
beyond and far beyond, a time of dark and light—the
trees and motels and a Shell gas station casino and the
distant orange skyline of a refinery and the tunnel of
treetops again—and he feels Kelly out there dying,
from pills he assumes, the fading away in a hotel room,
the haunting, and he's too late he's too late he is driving fast and he is too late and it would be better for
him just to turn the wheel just to embrace the silence

that he has always kept before his wife just to turn the wheel and fly into these trees and be silent forever but he bursts from the trees now and he races along the causeway the vast void of Lake Pontchartrain to one side and the Gulf to the other both horizons invisible in the far and utter dark, and it is all slow now, it is this encircling dark and the far-ahead razor-slash of the lights of New Orleans, and he feels as if he is not moving at all, though his mind knows he is moving fast, it is as if he were in a craft out in the great emptiness of space hurtling unspeakably fast but without a near point of reference and so seeming not to move at all, and he has no point of reference, he knows she is dying, and he will rush on like this forever rush in solitary trajectory between the stars, rush on without end: for he loves his wife he does love his wife and there is a long long way to go to get her back but he seems not to be moving at all and he wonders if he himself has died, if he is dead already.

~

And eighteen minutes later, Michael Hays slams to a stop in front of the Olivier House. He is out of his car and across the sidewalk and through the front door and at the far end of the entrance hall a woman rises from behind the desk and he strides toward her and he can see her stiffen and she is steady but for her hands that she struggles to keep from flailing in panic and Michael slides to his left to clearly put her out of his path, to head straight for the doors to the courtyard beyond.

"She's not here" Ramona says and he slips by.

"I'll call the police," she says.

"Do it," Michael says. "And an ambulance."

And he's through the doors and into the loggia and past the empty pool and he's going up the stairs two at a time pushing through an air thick with the ghosts of Kelly and Michael moving in this very space leaning into each other pausing once yes he held her here on this second floor landing and he kissed her and he turns and he presses hard gasping up one more floor now one more and he leaps these two steps and these two and these two and these two and he breaches breathless onto the third floor and Room 303 is before him and he pulls up and he squares himself and there are two narrow black doors in the frame with their upper panels glass and with the two knobs side by side in the center and he focuses on the spot between and just above the knobs and he lifts his right leg and he kicks and the door quakes but does not yield and he realizes he instinctively held back because of the glass and he is a fool and he senses a terrible silence inside the room and he raises his leg again and he kicks hard and the doors fly open before him and he strides over the shattering glass even as it still scatters and tumbles and the lamps are on and he strides and she is lying on her side at the far edge of the bed twisted there with her back to him and he strides and the room stinks and it is sweet to him it is hope to him she has rolled onto her side and has brought the pills up and he strides but was it enough and he is passing her and he looks down at her legs splayed on the bed and he knows the signs and her legs are white as the light he has pushed through the dark but her feet, her feet are blue, but it is a dusky blue and the paleness of the blue gives him hope and he is beside her and he sits and he turns her and he lifts her and with one hand he cradles her head and her eyes are open ever so slightly and he says "Darling please stay, please stay" and her eyes fall slowly closed and he says "It's Michael, my darling" and he waits for the eyes to open and they do not and he presses her to him and he is weeping now and he draws her away from him wishing he could show her his tears. But her eyes are closed, and he says "Kelly." And again he says "Kelly." And he says, "Kelly, please try to look at me." And her eyelids stir. And they begin to lift. And very slowly Kelly's eyes open. They open just a little and they stop, but she has opened her eyes.

And Michael says, "I love you. I'm so very sorry, my darling. I love you."

~

In the broad expanse of sunlight beneath the atrium in the West Lobby of the New Orleans Airport, Michael stops and looks hard into the dimness in the direction of the concourse. He was right. It's her, her flight is early. Sam drifts this way, looking about, and even as he sees her, she turns her face in his direction. Her face brightens and she waves and he lifts his hand to her and she rushes forward. He takes a step and another toward her and they are together in the middle of the sunlight and they embrace.

They stand very still and hold each other close, not saying a thing. And Michael lets his daughter decide when to let go. He lets her decide but he's glad she's prolonging this, he's glad to hold his baby in his arms. Then she gently pulls away and their hands go to each other's shoulders and they look into each other's eyes and he is very glad she has her mother's dark-of-the-night eyes.

"How is she?" Samantha says.

"She's fine," Michael says. "She'll be fine. She's threatening to bite off the tube down her throat."

"That's a good sign."

"Yes."

"And you, Daddy. How are you?"

Michael fights now. He fights off all the old impulses he has to shut up, to brush everything aside and just stay where he has always stayed, alone inside his head, lost but content in the woods. "Me?" he says.

"You," Sam says.

"I'm sorry," he says. "That's how I am. I'm very sorry."

"You didn't do this," Sam says.

"Sam," he says. He hesitates. But only because he has to push back the welling in him. He's not afraid now to show his tears to his daughter, but he wants to get these words out clearly.

She waits, searching his eyes. "Yes?" she says, softly.

"I love you," Michael says.

"Thank you, Daddy. I love you too."

"I've always loved you," he says.